"I'm her father?"

Maddie nodded, and tears filled her eyes. "I'm sorry. I gave you my number, but you never called..." She looked at him wide-eyed. "So I'm telling the truth. I have a daughter, and you are her father. And I promised her that if I ever found out who he was, I would tell her. So now I have to tell her."

A father. The one thing Luke had always said he'd never be, because he didn't know what kind of father he'd be.

"Are you sure?" he asked.

"Yes, but I'm willing to take a test if you want."

He believed her. He didn't need a test to do so.

"I always meant to call you," Luke said, "but I got into some trouble, and I couldn't. I'm sorry."

Now his mistakes that night seemed even worse than he'd ever thought.

A child.

He had a child.

Danica Favorite loves the adventure of living a creative life. She loves to explore the depths of human nature and follow people on the journey to happily-ever-after. Though the journey is often bumpy, those bumps refine imperfect characters as they live the lives God created them for. Oops, that just spoiled the endings of Danica's stories. Then again, getting there is all the fun. Find her at danicafavorite.com.

Books by Danica Favorite

Love Inspired

Shepherd's Creek

Journey to Forgiveness
The Bronc Rider's Twins
A Cowboy for the Summer
The Cowboy's Return

Double R Legacy

The Cowboy's Sacrifice
His True Purpose
A True Cowboy
Her Hidden Legacy

Three Sisters Ranch

Her Cowboy Inheritance
The Cowboy's Faith
His Christmas Redemption

Visit the Author Profile page at LoveInspired.com for more titles.

The Cowboy's Return

DANICA FAVORITE

LOVE INSPIRED
INSPIRATIONAL ROMANCE

LOVE INSPIRED®
INSPIRATIONAL ROMANCE

Recycling programs for this product may not exist in your area.

ISBN-13: 978-1-335-59874-5

The Cowboy's Return

Copyright © 2024 by Danica Favorite

Love Inspired
22 Adelaide St. West, 41st Floor
Toronto, Ontario M5H 4E3, Canada
www.LoveInspired.com

Printed in U.S.A.

But as for you, ye thought evil against me;
but God meant it unto good, to bring to pass,
as it is this day, to save much people alive.
—*Genesis* 50:20

For the real Luke and Stolley Bear.
Both gone too soon. We miss you.

Chapter One

Maddie Antere held back the urge to let out a squeal and give a fist pump as she walked out of her supervisor's office. Claire McCabe had been her supervisor for as long as Maddie had worked at the Shady Peaks Senior Center, from the time Maddie had found herself unexpectedly pregnant with her now eighteen-year-old daughter, Kayla. Claire had given Maddie a job when no one else would, and had helped Maddie navigate the ins and outs of the necessary schooling to do more than be a simple aide, so she could have more responsibilities and make more money.

And now…in just a few short weeks, as long as Maddie passed the review with the board of directors, when Claire retired, Maddie would be taking over Claire's job as the director of the center.

It seemed almost unreal.

For years, people had turned their noses up at Maddie, first because of the family she'd grown up in, and then becoming a single mom, and last but not least, all the mistakes she'd made on her own along the way. Maddie had told everyone that Brady King was Kayla's father despite it not being true, effectively ruining his life. Even though he had forgiven her and continued to prioritize her and Kayla as members of the family when the truth came out, Maddie had always felt like she'd never earned her place in this world. Sure, she helped out at Shepherd's Creek Stables and had even created a program for the seniors to be active there so they had more to do than some boring old crafts printed off the internet. But sometimes, she suspected her place there was given to her because they felt sorry for her, and, of course, for Kayla's sake.

But this…this was something Maddie had finally earned—through her own talents, abilities, and hard work.

All she had to do was keep up the good work she'd been doing all these years for one more month, and the recognition of being worthy based on her efforts was finally hers.

With a little spring of hopefulness in her step, she went into Ida Mae Christianson's room to begin her rounds for the day.

"Good morning, Ida Mae. Did you have a good breakfast?"

She didn't need to ask, since she knew that Ida Mae would likely complain about some aspect of the breakfast, and then launch into a long diatribe of how she could have a much better meal if she were allowed to go home and fix it herself.

But that was Ida Mae, and like all her residents, Maddie always took the time to listen and understand what the older woman was going through, because it was hard on people, not being in the homes they loved and were used to.

However, when Maddie stepped further into the room, she was greeted by the sight of a giant hulk of a man leaning over Ida Mae, brushing her hair with the soft hairbrush she loved tenderly.

"I sure did," Ida Mae said. "My grandson is finally here to visit, and he even brought me McDonald's for breakfast."

Maddie gave Ida Mae an indulgent smile. Though she did have a special preapproved menu to manage her health issues, even the dietician wouldn't be upset at a small treat once in a while. But she'd have to pull the grandson aside at some point to let him know this couldn't be a regular occurrence.

"That's so nice," Maddie said, smiling at the man. "I'm Maddie Antere, and I've been helping your grandmother. You must be the famous Luke I've heard so much about."

He stopped brushing his grandmother's hair to glance at Maddie, his warm brown eyes familiar, even though Maddie had never met this mysterious grandson. While Maddie had grown up knowing Ida Mae and most of her family, she'd never met Luke, whose father was in the military, so they'd always been traveling from post to post. From what Ida Mae had told Maddie, Luke had followed in his father's footsteps, so his visits to his grandmother were few and far between.

"It's nice to meet you," he said. "Granny speaks highly of you. I think if it weren't for you, she'd have burned the place down by now."

"I don't belong in here," Ida Mae said, sitting up straight in her chair "I'm not sick."

They also had this argument every day, but still Maddie smiled at her. "I know you're not. But the doctor says you have to stay here until your hip is fully healed so you don't end up here again. You know I love you, but I hope I never see you back here."

"You and me both," Ida Mae said, turning her attention to her grandson. "Maybe now that Luke is here, I can go home."

"Absolutely not."

Maddie turned to the sound of the voice behind her, trying not to groan. Briana Smith, Ida Mae's granddaughter who lived in town, who'd grown up with Maddie, and had often been a thorn in Maddie's side. The problem with having a troubled past in a small town was that people like Briana never let you forget.

She'd grown to dislike Briana's visits just as much as she'd disliked having classes with her in school. Briana always thought she was better than everyone else, and now, as the mayor's wife, the woman was even more intolerable. Every time Briana came, she found some fault in how Ida Mae was being cared for.

Hopefully, Luke wouldn't be as bad.

"Briana. Nice to see you," Luke said, stepping around the chair Ida Mae was in to greet his cousin.

But while he went in for the hug, Briana sidestepped him, giving him a dirty look.

"You should have let us know you were coming. Granny has a routine that shouldn't be disturbed."

"Yeah, a snooze fest," Ida Mae said. "Luke coming home is the best thing that's happened in years. He said he's staying for a while, so I can go home and he'll look after me."

Briana's eyes lit on the remains of the McDonald's breakfast. "I'm assuming he's the one who brought you that."

The smile on Ida Mae's face was brighter than any expression Maddie had ever seen on the older woman.

"My favorite."

"It's not on your diet," Briana said, then turned to Maddie. "Did you let this happen? I have made my expectations very clear in terms of my grandmother's care, and if you are falling short, I will have no choice but to speak to your supervisor."

Not only did Maddie receive this threat on a regular basis, but Briana had followed through multiple times. Every slight, real or imagined, got reported to Maddie's supervisor. Most of the time, Claire laughed it off and said it was no big deal, but with the promotion on the line, an official write up could put that in jeopardy.

"I only just arrived before you. We had just gotten through introductions, and then I was going to explain to Luke that while bringing your grandmother breakfast was a nice gesture, it's important to check with the dietician on any special treats he brings in."

Hopefully it would be enough to calm Briana down. When it came to her grandmother's care, Briana ran things with an iron fist. No wonder poor Ida Mae just wanted to go home. At least there, she didn't have to deal with Briana's nonsense all the time. But none of this was Maddie's business. She did her best to take care of Ida Mae while appeasing Briana.

"Who even let him in?" Briana asked.

Oh-kay… Maddie had heard that Luke was something of a black sheep. Prior to joining the military, he'd been in a lot of trouble, and even though it was years ago, Briana liked to remind everyone that she was the good grandchild and

Luke was the worthless one. Especially when Ida Mae got sentimental about her grandchildren.

"Anyone can visit any of the residents at any time during visiting hours, provided they meet the health requirements," Maddie said.

Briana turned her icy gaze to Luke, and Maddie felt a bit bad for him, because even though it got her out of the firing range, from what Maddie could tell, he was a loving grandson, so he didn't deserve this.

"Have you had all of your shots? I've heard the flu is going around," Briana asked.

Maddie forced herself not to giggle. It was like the other woman was talking about a dog going to a kennel.

"And then some," Luke said, squaring up against her. "With all the military travel I've done, I'm vaccinated against more things than you can possibly imagine, and I was given a clean bill of health before my discharge. I can assure you, you're likely more of a health risk to her than I am."

For a moment, Maddie stared at him for having the audacity to talk to Briana like that. Judging from Briana's indrawn breath, Briana couldn't believe it either. She was used to pushing everyone around and getting her way, no matter what the cost.

Luke winked at Maddie, and she couldn't help

smiling. Handsome and charming, plus standing up to Briana? A lethal combination, except that Maddie had sworn off dating a long time ago. In terms of men, Maddie had the worst judgment ever. In high school, she'd had a bad reputation with boys, even though she hadn't done anything with any of them until that fateful party when she'd gotten pregnant by some guy who'd given her a fake name and disappeared the morning after. Then, when she carried out the farce of trying to be with Brady to give Kayla a father, she'd only proven how inept she was at having a relationship with someone who was honestly trying to make things work, despite being in love with someone else. After that, she'd gone on a few dates, but all anyone ever saw was her reputation for being easy that she'd never actually earned.

No one would ever believe that she had only been with one person, one time, and it wasn't even that great. Actually, it was pretty terrible, but men just expected sex from her, so she said no thank you to it all. If all that garbage was what love and romance was about, you could count Maddie out.

Actually, she knew from observing her Shepherd's Creek family that there was a lot more to a lasting relationship than that, but with the way people in town looked at her, she wasn't sure it would ever happen for her.

Still, Luke was pretty cute, and he didn't know those things about her, so maybe…

Maddie shook her head. He was the grandson of a patient, and Briana's cousin, so that made it all completely inappropriate.

"We need to set some boundaries," Briana said.

Maddie felt her face heat, as if Briana had known her train of thought.

But then Briana continued, "I understand that you want to spend time with Granny while you're on leave. But it's very important that we keep to her schedule and make sure that there are no interruptions to her care that could bring on a setback. Your junk food treat could be harmful to her."

"I'm here to stay," Luke said. "They offered me a nice retirement package, and my friend Ken has a consulting business for veterans that he's asked me to join, so I'm taking his offer once I get Granny settled. I know you're busy with your son and your life, and I never had the chance to do any of that with all my travel, so when Granny broke her hip again when I got my offer, it was a no-brainer. It's time I fulfilled my family obligations. You can't take care of Granny, but I can."

Maddie had taken Kayla to Yellowstone once, and the expression on Briana's face was like a geyser about to go off. It was actually pretty funny, watching someone stand up to her, especially because in this case, there was nothing Briana could do.

"That's a lot of too little, too late," Briana said. "You haven't been involved in our lives in years. Now suddenly you appear? Given all your troubles over the years, I'm wondering what your motives really are and if your story is even true."

Ida Mae straightened in her chair and pounded on her table. "He video chats me every Sunday night, except for when he's doing secret work he can't tell me about."

That part, Maddie knew was true, because she'd helped Ida Mae get her tablet set up so she could chat with her grandson. Though Maddie had only heard "grandson" and had assumed that since Ida Mae hated the "great" reference, it was Drake, Briana's son who was in Kayla's class at school. And like his mother had done to Maddie, constantly tormented Kayla.

The joys of small-town living.

Where grudges ran long and deep. Which was why getting this promotion would finally prove that Maddie could break free of the past that everyone held against her.

"Like I said, I'm here to stay," Luke said. He pushed up his sleeves, like he was gearing up for battle, which was when Maddie noticed the tattoo on his forearm.

A snake, wrapped around a dagger, and the dagger's point was stuck inside an intricate heart.

She'd only ever seen one tattoo like it.

"Maddie, a word outside if you please," Briana said.

Maddie could barely process the thought as she nodded, her eyes still on the tattoo as she backed out of the room to listen to whatever nonsense Briana would go on about.

At the moment, Maddie felt like her heart was caving in. Just when she thought everything in her world was finally going right, the one thing that could destroy it all was happening.

Only one man had that same tattoo. Maddie had lovingly traced it the night of the party where Kayla had been conceived. He'd told her his name was Snake, like his tattoo, and he was only here to appease his family before going off to boot camp, but he was going to get out as soon as he could, and run away from their controlling ways, and make a life for himself.

Something about what he'd said had called out to her, and okay, they were both more than a little drunk. Maddie had thought it was something special, but he was gone the next morning, and she hadn't known where to find him. When she'd found out she was pregnant, she'd blamed Brady.

She'd always known Brady wasn't Kayla's father.

But for the first time, she knew who Kayla's father really was.

Luke Christianson, grandson of her favorite patient, and cousin of her nemesis.

As Maddie stepped out into the hall to receive the tongue-lashing Briana was going to give her, Luke felt bad for the woman who was just trying to do her job and was now caught between a rock and a hard place. It wasn't Maddie's fault that he and Briana had bad history.

Briana had hated him her entire life because she was jealous of him being the grandkid who lived far away and got spoiled whenever he came to visit. And then, of course, there was the night she never let him live down. His father had sent him to stay with his grandparents for the summer before he went off to boot camp, hoping that being in the small ranching community would keep him from doing anything stupid that would get him kicked out before he began. He'd gotten in some minor trouble back home, and his father was terrified he'd do something that would disqualify him from the army.

But one night, he'd had enough of the boredom, taken Briana's car, gone to a party, and gotten drunk. On the way home, he'd crashed the car into the ditch in front of their house and totaled it. Okay, there was way more to his side of the story than that, but that's all Briana knew, all she'd ever know, and all she cared about. Even though her dad had been angry, he'd also been pretty decent about the whole thing and not called the police. His dad had paid for the damages, then shipped him back home and pulled some strings to get him into boot camp early so he didn't do anything else to jeopardize his future.

To Briana, it was the worst betrayal, because in her eyes, Luke had gotten away with it. But the truth was, he hadn't. He'd sent every paycheck back to his dad until he'd paid off his debt, living in base housing, and doing everything as cheaply as possible to make up for what he'd done. Yes, he could have gotten arrested and put in jail for a DUI, which was still something Briana brought up as him deserving every time she could, but his dad had been right. Luke had never wanted to join the military, but it had done more to straighten Luke out than jail ever would.

He just wished he'd been able to thank Briana's dad for understanding that as well, but he'd died shortly after, and Luke had been deployed overseas and couldn't make it back for the funeral. Another thing Briana hated him for. He'd missed every major family event over the years. As a single man, he took the hazardous assignments that had him traveling the world so that the men with families didn't have to. Plus, he'd liked the connection to his family by saying he was a member of the cavalry division. His grandfather had served in the cavalry before becoming a rancher. While they only used horses for ceremonial purposes these days, he loved the pride in Granny's eyes when he'd say anything about being cavalry.

Unfortunately, Luke hadn't realized the cost to his extended family, especially his grandmother. Phone and video calls weren't enough to make up for his missing presence. Though he didn't like Briana's attitude toward him, she was right. He should have been here to help Granny.

The only reason Granny was in the senior center was that this was her second broken hip in a year, and both times she'd broken it because she was home alone, trying to do things she should have asked for help with. But now that Luke was out, he could be here for her, helping her so she didn't have to stay in this miserable place.

Okay, it really wasn't that miserable. Every time he talked to Granny, she went on and on about the nice people here, especially Maddie, but she hated having her days planned out, her meals tightly controlled, and constantly being pecked at by Briana. Granny had always been there for him, even when other family members had written him off. The least he could do was be there for her now.

"I do hope she's not being too hard on Maddie," Granny said, staring at the closed door. "Every time I break a rule and Briana finds out, she gets Maddie in trouble. One of these days, she's going to get that poor girl fired. I try to be good, but it's so hard following all the rules. I just want to go home."

That plaintive sigh killed him every time he spoke to her.

Though he wanted to believe that Granny would live forever, he had to be honest that she only had so many years left. The least he could do was spend those years making up for the ones he wasn't around. Granted, there were things he couldn't make up for, but he could do his best.

"I know, Granny, and when Maddie comes back, I'll ask her who I need to talk to so we can get the ball rolling. You're right, she seems really nice."

"And pretty," Granny added.

Not that again. Luke tried not to groan, but the expression on Granny's face told him she saw right through it.

"You've still got plenty of years left in you," she said. "Now you can get married and start a family. If you marry Maddie, you'll get a daughter, too, and Kayla is the sweetest thing. She comes to visit sometimes."

Luke shook his head. "I told you, no matchmaking. I'm perfectly happy with my life as it is, and I don't want your interference."

After all these years of being single, he was comfortable admitting that he was definitely not relationship material. The women he'd dated had complained about his military life, and that he could never share details on all the things he was doing. He might not be traveling now, but he still wasn't the type to give women the depth of emotion and whatnot that they all seemed to want from him. After being trained to stay closed for so long, he didn't know how to open up. Truthfully, he wasn't sure he wanted to. It seemed like every time he thought he was trusting someone, he got stabbed in the back.

He'd thought he was in love once. But all it took was a six-week deployment for him to come back to her messing around with someone else. Or that German woman he'd started dating, only to find out that what she really wanted from him was his money and a green card. If that was what romance was about, he'd pass.

"You just need to find the love of a good woman," Granny said, twisting her wedding rings on her finger. "Your grandfather and I had forty-seven years, and I still miss him every single day."

It didn't do him any good to remind her that these days, relationships like that were a rarity.

His parents might have been married for almost thirty years before his dad had passed, but he didn't have a lot of happy memories of his parents' marriage, since they were always fighting. His mom was remarried, but he didn't think much of his stepdad. It seemed more like she didn't want to be alone, as opposed to her finding someone she loved, who loved her back.

But nothing he said would satisfy Granny, so he patted her hand instead. "I wish all marriages were like what you had."

The door opened, and Maddie stepped into the room. "Sorry about that," she said. "Briana is talking to the director now."

The flat tone to Maddie's voice didn't encourage him. "Should I go have a word?" he asked.

She shook her head. "I'd wait until Briana leaves. She's got a nail appointment in an hour that she's stressed about getting to, so you can go then."

Then Maddie looked over her shoulder and back at him. "But please don't tell her I said so."

The bright, cheerful woman he'd met earlier had turned into a mouse. Despite telling Granny he had no interest in romance, he'd definitely agree with her assessment that Maddie was pretty. And Granny liked her, so that was a bonus as well. But he was definitely not interested in her, so he couldn't let his mind wander like this.

That said, he did feel bad that his presence was now causing trouble for her. Briana never seemed to care who she hurt, as long as she got her own way. And when she didn't, as in the case of Luke not going to jail for wrecking her car, she held the grudge forever.

"I do want to make sure that your boss knows none of this is your fault," he said. He glanced over at Granny, then added, "And I would like the information from the dietician so I can make sure that none of my treats are a threat to her health. I want to contribute to her care, not cause Granny harm."

The smile Maddie gave him warmed his heart, but he noticed it didn't fill her eyes, like she was still troubled about the situation.

"Seriously," he said. "None of this has anything to do with you. Briana has held a grudge against me for years, and she's taking it out on you. I'm truly sorry, and I will make sure that you don't face any repercussions."

His words didn't seem to make her feel any better. In fact, she looked even more agitated.

Finally, she said, "I know this is going to sound weird, but could I talk to you privately for a moment?"

So she was in trouble. Why did Briana have to be such a pain? But if she was going to make waves, then he'd do what he could to make things better for an innocent victim.

"Sure."

He followed her into the hallway, where she led him into a small conference room and closed the door behind them.

"Okay," he said. "You're scaring me. Granny isn't dying, is she?"

Maddie shook her head. "No. This is personal."

He stared at her. How could there be anything personal when they'd just met?

"Do you remember when you came home that summer before boot camp?"

Luke nodded. "Yeah. I take it Briana told you what I did?"

"No." Maddie wrung her hands in front of her. "Sorry. I didn't ever expect to have to do this."

"Do what?"

This woman was seriously weird. But something was clearly bothering her, and whatever it was, he'd hear her out.

"Do you remember going to a party?" She looked at the ground, shaking her head. "Sorry, you probably went to a lot of parties."

She didn't look up as she continued. "Anyway, there was this one party, and I met you, and…"

"I only went to one party," he said quietly. She didn't have to continue the story. He knew what she was trying to say. He'd met this great girl, they'd connected, and they'd…

"We did things I regret," she said really quickly, like she hadn't wanted to admit it, but felt that she needed closure. "And I ended up pregnant, which I don't regret, only I did other things I regret, but I promised myself and my daughter that if I ever saw her father, I'd find out his name, and I would tell her so that she would know who her father is."

Even though she spoke about a mile a minute, the words processed very slowly in his mind, almost like they were taking forever to form and didn't make sense.

And then it hit him.

"I'm her father?"

Maddie nodded, and tears filled her eyes. "I'm sorry. I gave you my number, but you never called, and you told me your name was Snake, and no one knew a Snake, and then I told a bunch of lies, so I didn't think it mattered, but then they all came out, so I promised that when I finally found out the truth, I'd tell the truth."

She looked at him, wide-eyed. "So I'm telling the truth. I have a daughter, her name is Kayla, and you are her father. So now I have to keep my promise."

A father. The one thing Luke had always said he'd never be, because he didn't know what kind of father he'd be.

"Are you sure?" he asked.

"I've only ever been with one person, but I'm willing to take a test if you want."

He believed her. He didn't need a test to do so.

"I remember that night," Luke said. "I always meant to call you, but I got into some trouble, and I couldn't. I'm sorry."

Now his mistakes of that night seemed even worse than he'd ever thought.

A child.

He had a child.

Kayla.

"How did you realize it was me?"

Maddie gestured at his tattoo. "You said you designed it yourself. It was your eighteenth birthday present to yourself, and you were really proud of it."

His heart thudded to the pit of his stomach. In all his earlier thoughts about opening up to women, he'd failed to include Maddie. The truth was, he'd opened up to her as well. That night, they'd connected in a very deep way. He'd shared things with her he'd never shared with anyone, and they'd been up most of the night, mostly talking. He'd thought it was something special.

But in the aftermath of his accident and everyone in the family being upset, he hadn't had time to call her. He'd asked Briana if she knew a girl named Maddie, and Briana had laughed and said the only Maddie she knew was no one worth knowing. Since Maddie was a common name, it hadn't occurred to him that all along, the Maddie he remembered was the Maddie they all had been talking about.

All this time.

She was right in front of him, and he hadn't known.

Worse, they had a child, who, based on when this had all happened, was essentially an adult now.

"She's what? Eighteen?"

Maddie nodded. "I don't want money or anything from you. We've done okay. I honestly never thought I'd see you again. But now, I have to do the right thing. My lies have cost me too much, and even though it might cost me even more, I need to tell the truth."

The woman was practically shaking, and while he was still reeling from the knowledge that he had a daughter, he wanted to reach out to her and tell her it was okay and comfort her somehow.

Yes, she'd made a mistake by having sex with him, but then, so had he. Somehow, they had to figure a way forward. Together.

Chapter Two

Maddie couldn't believe she'd done it. Even though she'd come clean about Brady not being Kayla's father a few years ago, it still felt like she'd had part of her lie hanging over her head because she hadn't been able to provide Kayla with her father's name. After watching the rest of the Shepherd's Creek family create their own versions of what family meant to them, which included bringing Maddie and Kayla into the fold despite Maddie's lies and having no blood connection to the family, she'd always felt guilty that she could never identify Kayla's biological father.

But why did it have to be Briana's hated cousin? Worse, her son Drake hated Kayla as much as Briana hated Maddie. And now they were family?

And here Maddie thought her life couldn't get any more complicated. Just once, she'd like God to make these lessons easy for a change.

She tilted her head heavenward and said silently, *Please?*

"I'm sorry to throw this all on you," Maddie said, looking at Luke again. "But I couldn't let this fester, not when it's been hidden so long. Because of my promise to Kayla, I have to tell her when she gets done with school."

Luke nodded. "She's a senior?"

"Yes. Already accepted to college. She's going to be a pediatrician because she loves kids."

A small smile lit up Luke's face. "So she's smart in addition to being a good kid who's nice to Granny."

She liked that Luke immediately picked up on Kayla's good qualities, as a proud father would do. "Yes. When she was little, I had to bring her to work sometimes because I didn't have childcare and didn't want to bug Brady, so they let me bring her as long as she didn't get in the way. She's always liked visiting the residents. Even as she got older, she liked to visit and entertain them."

Once again, he smiled, seemingly happy to have this insight into Kayla's positive qualities. It was probably good he learned these things about her before experiencing her bratty side, because she was still a teenager. And even the best teenagers could be trying at times.

"Who's Brady?"

Right. More facing her past.

"I was not a very good person back then,"

Maddie said, knowing that accepting this part of her was just as healing as anything else—at least, that's what her counselor told her. "I had a grudge with Junior, that is, Josie Shepherd, now King, and her boyfriend was there, and he was really drunk. I thought it would be funny to take pictures that made it look like we'd been intimate to cause problems between them. And then I discovered I was pregnant, and you were nowhere to be found, so I lied and said the baby was his. No one asked for proof, so everyone, including Brady, believed he was Kayla's father until she was almost fifteen."

Luke nodded slowly, and unlike everyone else who heard that story, he didn't look like he was judging her. "How did the truth come out? She wasn't sick or anything, was she?"

Again, Maddie had to give him credit for caring about a child he'd just found out was his. But it only made her feel worse, admitting what a despicable person she'd been.

"No, she's fine. Perfectly healthy." Maddie took a deep breath, then said, "Josie came back to town. She'd left because of my pregnancy and a falling out with her father, but he died, and he left the stables and his entire estate to her, so she came back. We had a fight, and the truth came out. I behaved very badly. Everyone seems to have forgiven me, but sometimes, I don't know if I can forgive myself. I hurt a lot of people."

All this time, Maddie had never thought much about what it would be like to face Kayla's father. She'd written him off as some guy at a party, without considering how he'd feel if he ever found out the truth. Granted, she hadn't known how to get in touch with Luke, or even know who he was, but the guilt was still there.

"I've done a lot of unforgiveable things, too," Luke said. "That's why I'm back. To make amends. I guess I have more amends to make than I thought. I should have called you. But I left you on your own to raise a baby and tell a lot of lies to cover up what we did. I'm just as responsible as you are."

He looked thoughtful for a moment, then said, "But Granny and I have been talking a lot about God, and what forgiveness means. Granny keeps telling me that God forgives me, so I should forgive myself. I guess we both need to learn that, so maybe we start by introducing me to our daughter, and facing those consequences."

It might be dumb to find comfort in his words, but all this time, part of her had been angry with him for abandoning her like that. And then she'd been angry with herself for being angry over him not being there for her because he didn't know, and she should have done more to figure out who he was. Why hadn't she been able to connect the dots that Ida Mae had a grandson visiting at the time? Probably because back then, she wouldn't have cared about some old lady and her visiting grandson. Unlike Kayla, who had an abundance of compassion, Maddie had not been that caring a person as a teenager.

Kayla was a reminder of the things Maddie had done right.

Funny how her daughter's example was what made Maddie want to do better and be a better person.

"If it's okay with you, I'd like to do this as a family for Kayla. After the truth came out, Brady and Josie insisted we be part of their family, and Kayla is very close to them. We're supposed to have dinner tonight as a family anyway, so maybe you could come, and I could tell everyone then?"

Even though she'd made it about Kayla, and it was true that Kayla would need their support, the truth also was, Maddie needed their support as well. Though Josie had once been Maddie's biggest nemesis, she was now one of Maddie's closest friends, as were Josie's cousins Abigail and Laura. Fortunately, Abigail and her husband were visiting from Minnesota, so it truly would be a family affair.

"Sure," Luke said. "Let me give you my number, and you can call with the details."

Though Maddie had a hard time seeing the rifts between her and Briana and Kayla and Drake mending, maybe this would heal their relationships as well.

But then Maddie looked out the window of the conference room she'd pulled Luke into. She saw Briana storming in their direction, Claire trailing helplessly behind her, and she wondered if it might take pigs flying first.

Briana threw open the conference room door. "What are you two doing in here?"

The last thing Maddie wanted was to have to tell Briana that Luke was Kayla's father before Kayla found out. As soon as Briana found out, the rumor mill would be hopping within minutes. Kayla didn't deserve that until she'd had time to process the news. Even then, she didn't deserve it, but it was inevitable.

That was the trouble with one lie. You think it's one little lie, but then it snowballs until it gains the power to hurt more and more people. And, in this case, the person Maddie least wanted to hurt in the world kept being the one hurt the most.

"We were discussing something private," Maddie said, hoping it was enough to calm Briana down long enough for her to come up with an excuse that wouldn't be a lie, but wouldn't share information she wasn't ready to share.

That was the other problem. Maddie had promised not to lie again, and so far, she'd kept that promise.

"This is highly inappropriate," Briana said, turning to Claire.

"Simmer down," Luke said. "This has nothing to do with Granny. Maddie thought she recognized my tattoo from all those years ago, and because she didn't want to get Granny excited with all her matchmaking nonsense, she wanted to ask me privately if I was the person she remembered."

Briana looked at them both suspiciously. "When would Maddie have met you?"

The expression on Luke's face was a lot like how Maddie felt. At least Luke could stand up to Briana without repercussions.

"The summer I wrecked your car. I was coming home from a party, which is where I met Maddie. We connected on a deep level. I'd promised to call her, and I never did, because of the car thing."

Instead of looking happy that they weren't conspiring about something having to do with Ida Mae, Briana glared at Maddie.

"So instead of taking care of my grandmother, which is your job, you decided to confront my cousin about ghosting you."

Briana turned to Claire. "And this is who you want taking your place?"

Maddie wanted to cry in frustration. But the few times she'd allowed tears to fall in front of Briana, Briana had weaponized them against her.

"Stop it," Luke said. "It's nothing like that. She was simply curious if I was the same guy or not. If you've been listening to Granny at all, you'd hear that she keeps telling me about every single woman she knows because she's desperate for me to settle down. I'm sure Maddie is getting the same, so it only makes sense to talk discreetly so no one gets Granny's hopes up. Unless you want Granny trying to set us up."

The shocked look on Briana's face both relieved and terrified Maddie. Clearly, Briana didn't want Maddie in the family anytime soon. But what was she going to do when she found out that Maddie's daughter was, in fact, Briana's family?

"We were about to go back to Granny," Luke continued. "So do you want to continue making a case out of nothing, or do you want to take care of her?"

"Fine." Briana gestured at the door. "After you."

As Luke stepped out of the room, Briana followed, but Claire hung back, motioning for Maddie to stay, then closed the door behind her.

"Look," Claire said. "I know that whatever private conversation you had with Luke was completely innocent. But you need to be on your guard right now. No more being alone with him or doing anything to give Briana the impression that you might be on his side. She thinks he's a danger to Ida Mae."

Maddie stared at her boss. "That's ridiculous. Luke isn't a danger to her. He loves her. She talks about him constantly."

"We need to stay out of their personal squabbles. And you need to stay away from Luke. Briana has the power to make both of our lives miserable, and she knows enough members of the board that she can keep you from getting this promotion."

Maddie knew Claire wasn't exaggerating. She had never seen such a grim look on her boss's face.

"But that's not fair to Ida Mae. I've never seen her so happy. We don't have the authority to interfere in that relationship without evidence he's harming her."

Claire shrugged. "He did bring her fast food, which is against her dietary restrictions."

Which people did for patients all the time, and they had meetings about it, and it was usually easily resolved.

"Luke asked me to set up a meeting with the dietician so he could understand Ida Mae's needs to make sure it doesn't happen again."

Maddie had followed protocol on this, and it seemed like Luke was willing to do the same, so it all should be a non-issue, except for Claire's concern.

Claire glanced at her watch. "I've got a meeting to get to, and you need to finish your rounds. We can talk later."

As they exited the conference room, Maddie felt like she had to throw up. She finally had the chance to make things right with her daughter, and tell the truth, but it might cost Maddie everything else she'd been working for.

Worse, a sweet old woman was being caught in the middle, and that didn't seem fair either.

So what was Maddie supposed to do? Any show of support for Luke, and she could lose her job. Even though the job itself was important to Maddie, there were also the people like Ida Mae that she genuinely cared for. If she got fired, she couldn't help them at all.

But all of that might be a moot point as soon as Briana found out that Luke was Maddie's father.

Whoever said that the truth would set you free had no idea just how rocky the path to freedom was.

Luke followed Briana into their grandmother's room, where Granny was watching a cop show and knitting one of her projects. All the years in the army, Granny would knit him things and send them to him, and when he'd mentioned his friends liked them, she'd started knitting random things for soldiers who didn't have anyone back home.

"What is this trash you're watching?" Briana asked.

"It's her favorite show," Luke said. Briana might take him to task for not being there, but at least he knew that their grandmother loved cop shows.

Briana glared at him.

"You are ruining our routine," Briana said. "We are supposed to go get our nails done. We have an appointment."

The frustration in her voice made him feel bad. Even though he did think she was being way over the top with her need to control, he hadn't thought about the plans she might already have that he was interfering with. He already knew that Briana wasn't his biggest fan, so he needed to tread lightly and give her space to accept that he was a different person now.

Maybe, if he eased her into the idea that he just wanted to be there for Granny, and even help lighten the load, they could come to a place of forgiveness.

"I'm sorry," Luke said, pulling out his wallet. "I didn't think about what plans you might have with her. Let me give you some money to cover the nails. Maybe take her out to a nice lunch, since you know what she can have. I know you probably have enough to cover it all, but let me do this for you as a way of saying I'm sorry."

At first, he didn't think she'd take it, but she grudgingly accepted the bills he handed her.

"Thank you," she said. "But don't think you can buy my affections."

He shrugged. "Not at all. I genuinely feel bad for not giving you warning and taking the time to work with your schedule. I was just excited to surprise Granny. Why don't you give me a call later today and we can work out plans so I can spend time with her without stepping on your toes? I'm here to stay, so let's figure out a way to work together."

Especially now that he knew he had a daughter here, leaving was the last thing he was going to do.

A daughter.

He had a daughter.

Even though he'd hoped to spend a good part of the day with Granny, maybe it was better that she and Briana had plans. He was still reeling from this new information, and he had to figure out what he was supposed to do.

What did you do when you found out you had a daughter after eighteen years? It wasn't like he could jump in and be a father. She was old enough that she didn't need parenting, so what was his role in her life?

He'd driven straight to the senior center to see Granny, and had planned on just staying at Granny's house, doing some of the work on it to make it more livable for Granny to come home. He was torn about getting a hotel so he didn't annoy Briana further by staying at the house. Now that he had a child, even an adult child, it seemed important to have a real home.

And then there was the complication of Maddie…

Granny had been pushing him a lot in that direction. What would she do when she found out that he and Maddie had a child together? At least Granny already knew and liked Kayla.

Kayla.

It was a nice name. What was her middle name? How had Maddie chosen it? Had she and Brady chosen the name together? The more questions he thought of, the more he wanted to know. This was his daughter, and it seemed almost surreal to think of himself as a father.

As he pulled up to Granny's house, it looked shabbier than he remembered. Gramps had been gone a long time, but surely Briana's husband, Corey, helped with the maintenance.

Still, he felt guilty because he should have been

here more to help. It was just easier to take another overseas assignment than to come home and face the consequences of the things he'd done.

It wasn't just the car. It was everything. The disrespect. The alcohol use. Stealing things from his family here and there to pay for it.

He'd thought that by following in his father's footsteps and joining the army, he'd finally make everyone proud, and it would make up for all the bad things he'd done. Granny was happy to see him, but Briana hated him. Luke's father was gone, but he'd died before Luke could ever hear the words, "I'm proud of you, son." His mother was remarried to some guy who preferred not to be reminded that she'd been married before.

So what else did Luke have?

A daughter.

In spite of all the things he'd done wrong, he had a daughter.

Who, by all accounts, seemed like a pretty great human being. He hadn't contributed to her life, other than some genetic material, but he was glad to know that at least she'd been raised well.

As he let himself into the house, he was horrified by the mess and disrepair. Granny had always been a meticulous housekeeper, but as he saw how things had gone unkempt, he could understand why everyone wanted her at the senior center so she could heal.

This was a way he could give back. Luke could clean up the house and fix all the things necessary for her to come home. He peeked into the main bathroom, which hadn't been updated since he'd left, and thought about how he could add some of those safety bars and things for older people. And as he passed from the kitchen to the dining room, he could see the step she'd tripped on while carrying a large box of junk and fallen and broken her hip. All of this, he could make safer for her so that when he talked to the doctor about her coming home, the doctor wouldn't be as concerned about her safety.

Maybe it would make Briana feel better as well.

He and his cousin didn't use to hate each other. Prior to that summer, they'd been the best of friends. But he'd hit his rebellion stage, and she'd remained Miss Perfect, and they forgot all the things they'd had in common.

Luke went into the room he'd stayed in when he'd visited. Still exactly the same as when he'd left. It wasn't like it was a special childhood room with his mementos, since it was just a basic guest room, but they hadn't changed anything in it.

He went to the floorboard where he'd created a hiding place and pulled it up, smiling as he saw the old box he'd hidden there. He opened it to find a half-empty bottle of vodka, which could go in the trash, a couple of crumpled dollar bills, and a folded piece of paper that brought back more memories.

He didn't have to examine it further. It was the paper Maddie had given him with her number. Funny that he still had it after all these years. Except it made him feel even worse that he had left her to cope with a pregnancy all alone.

But he'd been a hot mess back then, and according to her, she hadn't been that great of a person, either. Maybe it had been for the best, but it was hard to say.

His phone rang, and he didn't recognize the number, but he answered it anyway, in case it was one of Granny's doctors.

"Hi, it's Maddie."

Duh. Of course it was Maddie. He'd given her his number. And, unlike him, she was calling him to follow up.

"Family dinner is tonight at seven. Do you remember where Shepherd's Creek Stables is?"

"I do. You can't miss it driving out of town."

"Cool."

She sounded nervous, which was cute, but he hoped that the talk earlier of making sure no one thought there was anything romantic between them had gotten through. Wrangling his current life situation was hard enough as it was without having to throw in strange romantic feelings.

"Well, it's at the main house, so just show up and we'll see you then."

She hung up, but once again, it struck him how weird she sounded. He thought about Granny's matchmaking attempts. And then he realized how silly it was for him to automatically assume that bringing him into their lives would be easy. Of course she was nervous. She was about to tell her family and their daughter who he was. Anyone would be nervous.

Hadn't he already been stressing out about what he was supposed to do as Kayla's newfound father?

Should he bring a gift? If she was younger, he might get her a teddy bear or something, but even then, did kids even like stuffed animals these days?

He felt like he was failing at this father stuff already, and he'd only known he had a kid for a few hours.

The sight of flashing lights in front of the house interrupted his train of thought. Obviously, a neighbor had seen someone in the house and called the police.

Okay, then. Time to face that music, and then he'd figure out what to do with the rest of his life.

Chapter Three

Maddie's stomach was a ball of nerves when she opened the door to let Luke into the house. The rest of the family was gathered in the living room, chatting as they always did.

"You okay?" he asked, looking into her eyes, like they'd been friends forever and had only reconnected today. Aside from that one night, they'd hardly known each other at all.

And yet, something about having him here with her felt right, and that his concern for her gave her the strength she needed to nod.

"Yes. I'll feel better when it's over."

He reached forward and gave her a quick squeeze on the shoulder. "I know we barely know each other, but Granny constantly sings your praises, so I know that despite all your mistakes, you're still a good person. We have a child together, so no matter what, I'm going to be here for you to support whatever is best for her. I may not have been much of a father thus far, but going forward, I'm going to do whatever she needs."

His words brought tears to her eyes. As much as she'd been struggling all day, this small show of support gave her a tiny boost that made her believe things might turn out okay after all.

As they entered the room, conversation stopped. The family all turned to look at Luke.

"Hi, everyone. I want you to meet Luke."

Before she could continue, Kayla jumped up. "Mom! You finally have a boyfriend!"

Ouch. Kayla had been obsessed with the idea of Maddie finding someone, especially lately with the rest of their Shepherd's Creek family finding love. Maddie probably should have better prepared her daughter for this, but she wasn't sure how she was supposed to accomplish that.

"No." Luke stepped forward. "I'm your father."

Maddie cringed at the forwardness. She and Luke probably should have talked about how they were going to share the information rather than blurting it out like that. But at least the bandage was ripped off, so to speak.

If only her daughter didn't look like she'd been punched in the gut.

The silence of the others in the room told her that maybe she should have done a better job of preparing everyone.

Before Maddie could speak, Kayla said, "Well, then. Am I supposed to jump up and down for joy? What did you think would happen? I'd get all excited that finally my father is here?"

Kayla turned, like she was going to leave in a huff, but Maddie stopped her.

"Kayla!" Maddie turned to Luke. "I'm sorry. She's usually not this rude."

Some of the family murmured in the background, but Maddie was too focused on her daughter to hear what they were saying.

"She's entitled," he said quietly. "After all, where have I been her whole life?"

Remaining in her fighter stance, Kayla said, "You already know my questions, so why bother having a conversation? I don't need your answers."

"Kayla Mae," Brady said, gesturing at the couch. "Sit down and listen to what your father has to say."

"Which one?" she grumbled, doing as she was asked.

"You have every right to be angry," Luke said. "The truth is, I was a poor excuse for a human being when I met your mother. We had met at a party, she gave me her number, and I never called. There were extenuating circumstances, and I was off to basic training a couple days later, but that's no excuse. A decent man would have called. I am truly sorry for my actions. I should have been there for you and your mother, and I wasn't."

The humility in Luke's voice made Maddie want to reach out to him. But that would likely only stir Kayla up further.

"Mom says you gave her a fake name. Is that true?" Kayla asked.

Luke shrugged. "Yes and no. I had given myself the nickname of Snake, because I thought it sounded cool. I didn't realize until later that it was dumb."

"You said you went to basic training? How long were you in the military?" Kayla's stare remained hostile, and Maddie wished she could take her little girl in her arms and make it all better. But at some point in this conversation, that hostility would be directed at her as well.

"I just got out. My grandmother is in the care center your mom works at, so I came to visit her. Your mom recognized me, and she told me about you, then said she promised you that if she ever found me, she would tell you. So here I am."

Kayla looked thoughtful for a moment, then turned to Maddie. The pain in Maddie's stomach intensified as she hoped that she hadn't made a terrible mistake. "How did you recognize him?"

Maddie swallowed. An easy question at least. "His tattoo. He'd just gotten it when I met him, and he'd said he'd designed it himself."

As if he knew Kayla was going to ask, Luke rolled up his sleeve. "See?"

"So what am I supposed to do now?" Kayla asked.

Maddie sighed. "I don't know. But I'm keeping my promise to you. You get to do whatever you want with the information. I thought it would be easier to introduce him if the family was here to support you."

Judging from the way they all looked at her like she was crazy, Maddie wondered if she should have talked to the therapist they'd seen when the truth about Brady came out or something. But the weight of all the years of lies was heavy on her, and she'd thought this would be easier. Maybe that was where Maddie was still needing to grow. She'd thought about how it weighed on her, but not on Kayla.

"You don't have to call me Dad or anything," Luke said. "From what I understand, you already have a great dad. I don't want to take away from that or interfere. But I would like to get to know you, if that's okay."

Brady stood and held a hand out to Luke. "You are very welcome here. I don't know if Maddie told you, but we do family different from most."

He gestured at Josie. "This is my wife, Josie. Though I'm not biologically Kayla's father, I'm still Dad, and Josie is a bonus mom, but Kayla calls her Josie. Kayla calls our daughter, Shana, her sister."

The warmth in Brady's voice reassured Maddie and made her feel like everything was going to work out. He'd become the head of their strange family, and even though she'd initially gone about it the wrong way, she was grateful to have him in their lives.

"Let me introduce you to the rest of the family," Brady said. Then he gestured at Wyatt and Laura. "Laura is Josie's cousin, but they were raised as sisters."

For a moment, he hesitated, then said, "We don't make a big deal of it here, but I want to explain it so you understand that for us, family is much deeper than what most families are. Wyatt is Laura's second husband, and while the twins were technically fathered by her late husband, they're his boys, and they call him Dad. They named their baby boy Cash after her late husband."

Finally, he gestured at Abigail and Isaac. "Abigail is Laura's sister, and she raised both Josie and Laura. She's married to Isaac, and they live in Minnesota now. They're in the process of getting certified to adopt a kid from the foster care system. Who knows what that kid will call them, but regardless, he or she will be family."

Listening to Brady describe their family

warmed Maddie's heart. Sometimes it was easy to forget how they were all connected, and she welcomed the reminder that family looked however it looked, as long as it was full of love.

Brady turned to her, and she appreciated the way he looked at her—as a friend, and even after all this time, an equal partner in parenting Kayla.

"As for Maddie," Brady added, "yeah, she came to our family in an unusual way, but without her, Kayla would not be part of this family, so we choose to love and accept her as our family. Whoever she chooses to add to the family, they become our family, too."

Brady had given her this speech a few times, but it still never failed to bring tears to Maddie's eyes. Though she never loved him in a romantic way, he and Josie provided an example of what she hoped for in finding love for herself. And, if Maddie were honest, she'd come to love Brady as a trusted brother and friend. Even though this was news to everyone else here, Maddie had called Brady and told him what was going on. Though he must have been feeling a wide variety of emotions now that Kayla's biological father was in the picture, Brady was handling the situation with the same kindness and ease he did everything.

Then Brady looked Luke in the eye. "You are Kayla's biological father, and therefore, you are family now, too. Sure, we have stuff to work out. But when she's not upset at having new information thrown at her, Kayla's a pretty good kid, and you'll enjoy getting to know her."

Josie tugged at Brady's hand. He looked down at her, grinned, then addressed the group. "And, since we have everyone together, and so we can take some pressure off Kayla, we might as well let you all know, we're expecting another baby."

As the room burst into excited chatter, Maddie felt the tension leave her body. Doing this as a family had been the right decision, because Brady had managed to make it easier on everyone.

Maddie turned to Luke. "Well, welcome to the family. Now come help me finish getting dinner on the table."

As they all made their way into the kitchen, Maddie noticed Brady pushing Kayla in Luke's direction. The poor guy looked overwhelmed and nervous as all get-out, but fortunately, Kayla noticed, too.

She held out a hand to Luke. "Hi," Kayla said. "I'm Kayla, and I'm kind of a jerk sometimes, but my dad says I'll eventually grow out of it. Mostly, though, I try to be nice."

Maddie laughed, and Josie put an arm around her. "It's going to be okay. He and Kayla will be friends in no time."

Maddie gave Josie a squeeze. "I hope so. Ida

Mae thinks the world of him, so I have to trust that I didn't make a mistake in bringing him into Kayla's life. And look at you! Another baby! Congrats!"

Josie gave a weak smile. "Thanks. I have way more morning sickness this time, so I don't yet have the energy to be excited, but the doctor says everyone is healthy, so I can't ask for more."

"Healthy is all we care about," Maddie said, smiling.

"Did you say that he's Ida Mae's grandson?" Abigail asked, joining them. "I heard that he was back and creating a stir. I guess we're about to add to the pot."

Luke obviously overheard and hung his head, and Maddie felt bad for him. After today's mess at the senior center, and his comments about wanting to make up for past mistakes, he was probably feeling overwhelmed. At least that was something Maddie could relate to. She'd spent so much of her life being the outcast that she understood his pain.

Which put Maddie in an even more precarious position. This man was the father of her child, so she owed it to them all to have a good relationship with him. Given their similarities in having compassion for Granny, she could see where it would be easy to work with him as a co-parent. The trouble was, getting close to him could mean endangering the career she'd worked so hard for, if Briana had anything to say about it.

On one hand, it should be easy enough to choose family over career. On the other, why should she have to choose?

And yet, seeing the pain and regret on Luke's face told Maddie that this wasn't going to be an easy road.

"I forgot how fast gossip travels in small towns," Luke said. "For those who haven't heard, Briana had me arrested for breaking into Granny's house today."

Maddie knew that Briana was cold, but that seemed a bit too cold, even for her. "What happened?" she asked.

Everyone was looking at Luke, who shook his head slowly. "I went to the house to see what I could do to fix it up to get Granny home eventually, and Briana saw me there and called the cops to say someone was breaking into the house. Thankfully, Granny was able to corroborate that she'd given me the key, but they cuffed me and everything. I'm pretty sure Briana took photos to frame."

"She is so difficult," Abigail said sympathetically. "I'm sorry you went through that. Is everything okay now?"

Luke nodded. "Yes, and it makes me more determined to fix up the house so Granny can come home. No offense to the senior center, but it seems like they're doing everything they can to make sure I get as little time as possible with Granny."

He looked over at Maddie as he spoke, and Maddie wanted to crawl under the table. "I'm sorry," she said quietly. "Briana met with my boss, and she's determined to cause trouble for you. I don't know why she's so threatened by you. Your grandmother constantly talks about you and how much she loves you."

"Wait a second," Kayla said. "I love Ida Mae. Sometimes I go in there and she tries to teach me how to knit, but I'm terrible at it. That's so cool that she's actually my grandmother. I always thought it was neat that we had the same middle name. Now it's even more special."

"Great-grandmother," Luke corrected her. Then he turned his attention back to Maddie. "I had wondered where her name came from. I love that she has Granny's same middle name, even though it was unintentional."

Before Maddie answered, Kayla said, "Mom and Dad both liked the name Kayla, and Mae was for Mom's grandmother, Mae, who Mom said loved her the best of anyone in her family. I like that I'm named after both of my great-grandmothers, since they both have the same name."

And just like that, the ice between her daughter and Luke was finally broken. They started chattering about Ida Mae, and Kayla's excitement at being related to her, and it seemed like everything would be okay between them.

Though Maddie had a million reasons why it was a bad idea, she couldn't help thinking how attractive Luke was, smiling and talking animatedly with her daughter. That was the other reason Maddie had never dated much. Since she was born, Kayla was the most important thing to Maddie, and she'd never found a man who was willing to connect with her daughter the way Luke was doing now.

But even if Maddie was open to dating, Luke needed this time to focus on his relationship with Kayla, not start something with Maddie.

By the end of the evening, Maddie was feeling better about the situation. Her daughter knew the truth, had met her father, and aside from a few snarky comments, it had been mostly smooth sailing.

Maddie had offered to do the dishes so the people with little ones could get them home and to bed, and so Luke and Kayla could have time together. As she was putting the last of the dishes away, Kayla came into the room.

"Luke is getting ready to leave, so I thought I'd let you know if you wanted to say goodbye."

Maddie wiped her hands on a dish towel. "Thanks. I hope you had a good chat with him."

Kayla shrugged. "He seems nice. But gross, that means I'm related to the Smiths. That's going to be fun when Drake finds out we're related."

Then she smiled. "Luke said he'd meet up with me after school tomorrow, and we can tell Granny together that we're related."

Just like that, the bubble of hope was burst. While telling Ida Mae about Kayla was the right thing to do, it also meant Briana would find out. Which meant that Maddie had until Kayla got out of school tomorrow to figure out a way to let this news be known without it destroying everything she'd ever worked for.

God, I know I've made a lot of mistakes, and I don't deserve the kindness I've been given. But please, help us get through this without me losing my job.

As far as prayers went, it wasn't the best or most elegant. But Maddie wasn't known for her wisdom and talent when it came to communicating with God. She could only hope that God could see how truly sorry she was for all the bad things she had done, and that she was desperately trying to make them right. Maybe God could give her a break here. Not just for her sake, but for Kayla's, Luke's, and even Ida Mae's.

Luke felt more confident the next day as he entered Granny's room. He'd called a lawyer about the situation in the senior center, and they'd told him that legally, Briana didn't have the right to exclude him from seeing Granny. The center could not prevent him from seeing her, either. Unless they had a legal reason for denying him access, or Granny did not want him there, blocking him from seeing her was against the law.

Granny was sitting in her favorite chair, knitting as she watched her favorite police show. However, when she heard Luke, she abruptly shut it off and turned to him, then laughed.

"Sorry, I thought you were Briana."

Luke laughed with her. "Why do you care about Briana's disapproval of your television shows? They make you happy."

The crestfallen look on Granny's face made Luke go over to her and take her hand.

"It's just easier to agree with her. She's always been a disagreeable person, and she and her family are the only family I have left."

Luke gave her hand a squeeze. "That isn't true anymore. I'm here for you, and this time, I'm not going anywhere."

As Granny smiled at him, Luke was once again relieved that he'd made the decision to come here. It also strengthened his resolve to fix up Granny's house so she could come home. She'd had a good, long life, and she deserved to spend all the days she had left enjoying it.

"You remind me so much of your father," she said. "The trouble with him was that he had a devotion to his country that his family couldn't compete with. I'm glad that you've seen the importance of family before it's too late."

Her words struck a chord he hadn't expected. He'd spent so much of his life trying to prove himself worthy of his father that it seemed funny to hear how much like him he was. He thought his actions had come out of devotion to his family, but now he could see that it was more of a devotion to his insecurity than anything else.

But that only made telling Granny that he had a long-lost child more nerve-racking. Family was everything to her, so how was she going to react to being denied this for so long? His palms were sweating as he waited for Maddie and Kayla to arrive.

"What's going on?" Granny asked. "You're acting mighty suspicious."

He'd never been able to hide much from Granny, which was why it was funny he thought he'd gotten away with so much as a teenager. Maybe that was why it was important to him to make things right with her. She'd always been the one who had loved him unconditionally, even when he'd done stupid things.

He shook his head and chuckled to himself as he remembered the time he'd found her stash of cash she'd been saving. He'd planned on using it to take a bus to get out of there, but when he'd tried to sneak out in the middle of the night, Granny was sitting there in her chair, calmly knitting a blanket, and told him that if he needed more money, her purse was on the table.

He hadn't been able to go through with it. He'd come up with some lie he couldn't even remember now and gone back to his bedroom. The next chance he'd gotten, he'd returned all the money he'd taken. So now when she gave him the same look she'd given him that night, he wanted to tell her everything.

"I promise, Granny, it's good news. I just need a little more time to tell you, so please be patient."

Granny grinned. "I've still got it, don't I? I can still sniff out subterfuge."

He laughed. "You sure do."

Then she gave him a conspiratorial look. "Did you bring me any chocolate?"

Luke shook his head. "I'm not going to fall for that this time," he said. "I met with your dietitian to find out what you are and aren't allowed to have."

Granny scowled. "I knew I shouldn't have signed those forms to give you permission to look at my private stuff. It's bad enough I've got to be stuck in this place, but everyone's conspiring against me to not have any of the good things in life."

Luke tried not to laugh, and shook his head at her instead. "We're only doing this because we love you."

Granny snorted. "If you love me, then break me out of this prison."

Just then Maddie walked in, and Granny looked even more perturbed. "No offense to you. You're not that bad. You should bring that daughter of yours to come visit me."

Which was when Kayla entered the room. The scowl left Granny's face.

"Finally something good is happening today," Granny said.

Luke looked over at Maddie. "She's upset with me because I didn't bring her any chocolate. Now that I know what her dietary restrictions are, she's annoyed at me because I'm not breaking the rules."

He loved the way Maddie smiled at him, then at Granny. She was such a wonderful woman. He was really grateful that as the sins of his past caught up with him, she was the mother of his child.

"Ida Mae, I've told you that there are alternatives that taste just as good. I'll get you some tonight and bring them over to you tomorrow."

Granny scowled at her. "That stuff tastes like

cow manure. All the fake sweeteners and all that supposedly healthy stuff tastes like garbage. What's wrong with a potato chip?"

Maddie gave her another gentle smile. "Even the low-sodium ones have too much salt. If you'd gone to our healthy snack class, you would have seen the demonstration of how we can use a dehydrator and turn vegetables into a crunchy chip."

Luke tried not to laugh at the disgusted look on Granny's face.

"No one is ever going to convince me that kale is a delicious snack."

Maddie shrugged. "You might think so, but when I make my kale chips, Kayla and all of her friends eat them as soon as I get them out of my dehydrator."

Granny looked over Kayla. "If you break me out of this joint, I promise, we will have the biggest junk food feast of your life, and you'll see what you've been missing out on."

Kayla shrugged. "I know it makes me a weirdo, but I like my mom's healthy snacks. I've never been into sweets, so as much as I hate to say it, you're not getting any help from me."

While Granny was seemingly looking for a new retort, Luke chose to take this as his opportunity to speak.

"Remember you said that you thought I was hiding something from you?"

Granny glared at him. "Oh, I know what you're doing. You're just distracting me from finding out what Kayla's weakness is to use to bribe her to bring me snacks." Then she grinned. "But I'll allow it. I do love a good secret."

Luke took a deep breath, then gestured at Kayla. "Granny, Kayla is my daughter."

Granny made a face and stared at him. "Oh, come on. I might be an old fool, but I wasn't born yesterday. Your attempt at a practical joke isn't going to trick me."

Maddie stepped forward and gave Kayla a little nudge in Granny's direction. "It's true," she said. "Kayla is Luke's daughter."

The shock on Granny's face was quickly replaced with curiosity, and maybe a touch of happiness. It always bothered her that Luke never married and had children and that Briana had only chosen to have one.

"Why didn't you tell me about this before?" Granny asked.

Maddie shrugged, then laughed. "Because I didn't know before. When I met Luke, he told me his name was Snake. We'd only met once before he disappeared."

Luke swallowed as he looked at Granny. He'd have to bring up that horrible night, but it was the right thing to do. So Granny understood they weren't deliberately keeping secrets from her.

"It was the night that I stole Briana's car and went to that party. I met Maddie, and, well, you know what happened after I got home. It wasn't like I could stay in touch with her."

Granny nodded thoughtfully. "I've never seen your father and grandfather so angry. And Briana's father. It wasn't even that great of a car."

Trust Granny to tell it like it was. Then she stared at Maddie. "How did you figure out Luke was the father?"

Maddie gestured at Luke's forearm. "His tattoo. He said he designed it himself. I knew it was unique. When I met him yesterday, I recognized it immediately."

Granny made a noise. "That ugly thing. I always said there was no reason for a person to mark up a perfectly good body like that."

Then she looked over Kayla. "But I suppose, since it has finally brought my great-granddaughter to me, that ugly thing wasn't so bad after all."

Then Granny held out her arms. "Now come here and give me some love. I've hugged you before, but it was before I knew we were family. So that means I've got a lot of hugging to make up for. I do hope you're a hugger."

Maddie leaned into him and whispered, "Kayla is actually not a hugger, so the fact that she's hugging your grandmother right now is a really big deal."

Kayla must've heard her mother, because she looked up at her and said, "Yeah, so get used to it. I'll give her hugs instead of drugs in the form of sugar and junk food."

They all laughed at Kayla's pronouncement. He'd known that Granny would accept Kayla, but he'd been afraid that she might get really angry with him.

Once Kayla finished hugging Granny, Granny said, "So, that's it? That's what had you all nervous?"

Luke nodded. "I know I did a lot of things during that time of my life that I am not proud of, and I came here hoping I could make up for it, but it feels like I just keep being presented with more and more of my mistakes."

Granny gestured at Kayla. "I would never call this beautiful girl a mistake. While I would've liked to have been part of her life sooner, I've at least had the privilege of getting to know her over the years, and I couldn't be more thrilled to find out we're related."

Granny smiled at Kayla, then said, "Even if you are one of those health food weirdos."

Granny adjusted herself in her chair. "Now get me my cell phone. I need to call my lawyer and get him to change my will."

Luke glanced over at Maddie to see if she understood what a big deal this was. Granny hated her cell phone, and she also hated parting with her money. So for that to be Granny's first response after accepting Kayla, it truly did mean everything was going to be okay.

The frustration on Maddie's face was obvious, and Luke could understand why. He'd been dealing with Briana and her suspicions about him trying to take Granny's money, and it was offensive. He had plenty of money of his own. Even with his plans to fix up her house, he was going to use his money, not Granny's.

"That's very kind of you," Maddie said. "But please don't make any rash decisions. Kayla and I are fine, and we don't need anything from you, other than a relationship."

The sincerity in her voice brought even more comfort to Luke. She'd told him the same thing, yet he did feel like he needed to contribute to Kayla somehow. But that was a conversation for a later time.

"I have more money than I know what to do with," Granny said. "I can't take any of it with me to the grave, so why not give some of it to Kayla?"

The stubborn set to Granny's jaw told him that Granny was going to do this whether Maddie agreed or not.

Granny looked at Kayla. "What are your plans for college?"

Kayla shrugged. "I've gotten accepted to a few, so I'm applying for scholarships."

Granny looked over at Maddie. "What's in her college fund?"

The distressed look on Maddie's face made him feel bad for her. There likely wasn't a college fund, and when they had a private moment, he would make sure Maddie understood he would contribute his share. Actually, more than his share, because Maddie had supported their daughter her whole life. It was his turn to step up.

Before Maddie could answer, Kayla said, "My parents have worked hard their whole lives just to keep a roof over my head. That's why I'm applying for some scholarships. I've studied hard to get good grades and done all the things scholarship people look for in a worthy recipient."

Granny looked at Kayla, then at Maddie, then back to Kayla. "You keep me posted on those scholarships. When the time comes, I'll make sure you've got enough money to go where you want, because this is your future we're talking about."

"What are you saying?" Briana asked, bursting into the room. "Why would you give this child your money for college?"

Then she looked over at Maddie. "This is your doing, isn't it? That's the real reason your daughter has been coming here to interact with all the seniors. It's not to keep them company. It's to take their money."

"Now, wait just a minute," Luke said, feeling the heat in his face rising as he watched his daughter shrink back uncomfortably. "How dare you walk into the middle of the conversation and make wild accusations? I've barely met them, and I know they have more integrity than to do something like that."

Briana glared at him. "And yet here we are."

Maddie held out her hands. "Whoa. Let's get something straight. First of all, I have never asked anyone, least of all Ida Mae, for money for college or anything else. You just walked in on Ida Mae offering, too soon to hear me refuse, but here I am, refusing."

Maddie looked over at Ida Mae and gave her a warm but firm smile. "That is very kind of you to think of Kayla, but I'm afraid we will have to turn down your generous offer. It wouldn't be appropriate."

Instead of appeasing Briana, she only glared at Maddie. "So you say. I'm going to be watching my grandmother's finances just to make sure you aren't getting anything."

Maddie looked distraught at her words, and Luke didn't blame her. After all, Maddie had never done or said anything to give any indication that she would do something like that, especially since she'd already been insistent that she didn't want anything from him financially, and he was Kayla's father.

Maddie squared her shoulders. "You are welcome to do so. You won't find anything wrong. In fact, because there are so many safeguards preventing employees of senior care facilities from accessing their residents' finances, there's a better chance of me embezzling from the federal government than accessing any of your grandmother's money. I don't want her money or anything else from her, other than her friendship."

Given that Luke wanted to wring his cousin's neck, he had to give Maddie double credit for being so kind to Briana. But again, rather than acting appeased about the situation, Briana marched over to the nurse call button and pressed it.

"What are you doing?" Maddie asked. "I'm right here. What do you need for your grandmother? I'll take care of it."

"I want the supervisor," Briana said. "It's very clear that you should not be anywhere near my grandmother, and even though I was assured yesterday that you would not be a problem, it's clear that you *are*. I told you to stay away and not to interfere, so now you will face the consequences."

The fear on Maddie's face made Luke wish he could do more for her. His cousin was a bully, always had been, and this wasn't right. He could tell by the way Kayla hovered close to her mother that this was upsetting for her as well. Unfortunately, since he barely knew his daughter, he wasn't sure how to reassure her.

One of the nursing assistants entered the room, appearing a bit frazzled. "What can I help you with?"

"Get the director," Briana said.

The aide looked over at Maddie, seeming confused.

"I know you're really busy," Maddie said, "but Briana isn't going to be happy until Claire has been brought into the situation. Can you please get her?"

The aide nodded, giving Briana a terrified glance, and it occurred to Luke that Briana probably terrified all the staff here. Not just Maddie. He already talked to a lawyer to make sure that his rights were protected, but maybe it wouldn't be a bad idea to get some advice on making sure that Granny was also protected. Not that he thought Briana would do anything malicious to Granny, but he had to wonder if Granny was getting the best care from people if his cousin was constantly bullying the staff. One more reason for him to get her house ready for her as soon as possible.

Briana glared at Maddie. "That was brave of

you, asking for your boss. You realize that you're going to be fired, right?"

Maddie looked defeated. Luke wished he had the kind of relationship with her that he could give her a hug and tell her it was going to be okay. He didn't even know that for sure, but he did know that Maddie had done nothing wrong, and it wasn't fair that his cousin was treating her like this.

Even though he hadn't discussed with Maddie or Kayla who else was going to know about their relationship, he said, "Stop this. There is a very good reason why Granny was offering money for Kayla's college."

Then he looked over Granny. "But it won't be necessary, not because I'm bothered by Briana's threats, but because she is my daughter, and I will be paying for it."

As petty as it was, he wished he'd had a video of Briana's gasp and stunned expression.

"That's not true," Briana said.

"It is true," Luke said. "Kayla is my daughter, conceived the night I went to that party and wrecked your car."

It was so worth it to see the shock on Briana's face. But she quickly recovered, then said, "Maddie has already lied about who fathered her baby, so she's probably lying to you, to get her hands on your money and Granny's. Maddie keeps telling everyone she's changed and she's a Christian and she's working to make up for all the bad things she's done. But here she is, lying about her child's father, yet again, to get money out of a helpless old woman."

"I'm not lying," Maddie said. "I know you have every reason not to believe me, but this is the truth. And if Kayla and Luke are in agreement, I am happy to have a paternity test done. I know who her father is, and it's Luke."

She looked like she was ready to cry, and Luke wanted to put his arms around her, but then her supervisor came into the room. "What's going on in here?"

Briana glared at Maddie. "I demand that you fire this woman," she said. "She's trying to take advantage of my grandmother by lying and saying that Kayla is Luke's daughter. I want her gone."

Claire appeared calm, then said, "Maddie, can you please explain?"

A tear rolled down Maddie's face. Then she crossed her arms over her chest and said, "I realize this is a strange situation, but after meeting Luke yesterday, I realized that he is Kayla's father. I didn't intend for it to come out this way, but it was important for Luke to let his grandmother know who Kayla was. I just want to tell the truth."

"And take all of Granny's money," Briana said.

"Stop!" Kayla said, tears running down her face. "Why won't you listen to my mom?"

Granny, who had been watching the whole scene with interest, grabbed her cane and pounded the table with it. "That's enough. Maddie says that Luke is Kayla's father, and based on the circumstances that are known to me, I believe her. Maddie did not ask for money. I offered."

Then Granny pointed her cane at Maddie. "And she refused, but it's my great-grandchild, and I'll do what I want."

A tender look crossed her face as she brought her gaze to Kayla. "I don't want you worrying about all this adult nonsense. You are my family, and I love you, and that is that."

Luke's heart felt lighter as his daughter wiped the tears from her face with her sleeve and nodded.

Maddie turned to Claire, looking anxious. "I promise, I did not ask for anything, and I will refuse anything that is offered. I don't want her money. I didn't tell Luke about Kayla because I wanted his money. I just want the truth to be known."

Claire nodded. "All right, then." She looked over at Granny. "I don't want to have to keep dealing with these scenes, and I'm doing the best I can in the situation. I understand that you have just received some interesting news. However, with your heart condition, it's also good for you to not get so excited. I'm going to have one of the nurses come in and make sure that you haven't suffered any ill effects from this new-found knowledge."

Then she turned her attention to Luke. "As I told you yesterday, your grandmother's health and safety is my primary concern. I know you want the best for her, but since you've come, there's been more excitement in her life than she needs. So you, me, Maddie, and Briana are going to have a little chat in my office, and we're going to figure out how to create the best environment for Ida Mae's healing."

Then she glanced at Kayla. "I know you're a regular visitor here, and everyone loves having you. But for today, I'd like you to go home while we figure out the situation."

Granny scowled. "Don't I get a say in all this?"

The director smiled at Granny. "Yes, you do. However, with the way everyone has been acting, and since I was called in here to deal with the situation, I need them all on the same page. Then you and I will talk about how to make this work for you."

Luke smiled at the director. Ultimately, he wanted what was best for Granny, and he appreciated that the director was going to be considering Granny's needs and desires.

"Good." Granny stared at the director. "Can we also discuss giving me some food with flavor?"

Everyone in the room except for Briana laughed.

"I can't change your diet," Claire said. "But I will talk to the dietitian about trying some new things with you that might make you feel better."

Then Claire looked at each of them. "But for now, I'm going to sit everyone down and we're going to figure out what's going on, and come up with a plan to move forward."

Even though he felt a lot like he was being called into the principal's office, Luke meekly followed her out of the room. He knew Granny was going to be okay, but after some of the things Briana said, Luke was now concerned about Maddie and her job.

Chapter Four

Maddie took a sip from the steaming coffee as she sat in her truck, waiting for Luke and Granny to arrive at the stables. Since finding out that she was related to Granny, Kayla had been to the nursing home to visit her father and great-grandmother every day. Now that Kayla and Granny knew about their relationship, both wanted to be more active in each other's lives.

Though Granny had seen Kayla ride countless times before at community events, she'd never done so with the knowledge that Kayla was her great-granddaughter. So today, Luke was bringing Granny out to watch her practice, after having obtained permission from Granny's doctors to allow her to leave. At this point, her stay at the senior center was largely due to safety concerns. While a home nurse could theoretically check in on Granny and she could be driven to and from her PT appointments, Granny's house still wasn't safe enough for her to stay in, even with Luke's help. Hopefully, soon, with the renovations he was doing, she could go home.

And then, they could put all the mess with Maddie's job behind them. Maddie took another sip of her coffee. She was exhausted from having to be at work all night, and had only had a couple hours' sleep before coming to the stables to watch Kayla ride.

In order to keep the peace, Maddie's shift had been changed to nights so that she would avoid any unpleasant encounters with Briana. It felt incredibly unfair having to move her life around like this. But as Claire reminded her, Maddie had to keep her eye on the prize and do what was necessary to get through the next couple of months as the board reviewed qualified candidates to take Claire's position.

Though Briana didn't have the legal right to control who did and didn't get to see Granny, Claire had suggested that it would be best for everyone involved, especially given the spotlight on Maddie, for Maddie to lay low for the time being. And, despite the fact that they all knew there had been no wrongdoing, Claire wanted to protect Maddie.

When Luke's black SUV pulled up, Maddie stepped out of the truck and waved them over. As much as she had been trying to fight her attraction to Luke, she couldn't help noticing how good he looked today, wearing simple jeans and a T-shirt. Nothing special, but it was the way he held himself. Every day that passed since finding out that Kayla was his daughter, he stood a little taller and walked with more of a spring in his step. The way he went over to Granny's side of the car and helped her out and got her situated with her walker made Maddie's heart skip a beat. Even though she'd call him handsome, her attraction to him was more about him being kind.

In all her years at the senior center, Maddie hadn't met many doting grandsons who cared for their grandmothers the way Luke did. Briana might think that Luke had ulterior motives or was trying to get something out of Granny, but Maddie had run into a number of those people in her time, and there was no way she could believe that Luke was one of them.

"Dad!" Kayla came running out of the stables with a smile on her face. "Granny!"

Kayla hadn't started calling Luke "Dad" until she'd talked to Brady and made sure it wouldn't hurt his feelings. Brady would always be Kayla's dad, and now she had another one.

"Hey, kiddo," Luke said, holding out his arms and receiving a big hug from his daughter.

The crunch of boots on the gravel behind Maddie made her turn. Brady.

"Hey," she said.

He nodded at her. "Hey."

She couldn't read the expression on his face, but she could tell he was watching Kayla and Luke intently.

"You sure you're okay with this?" she asked.

Brady nodded. "From day one, we both said that we wanted the best for our daughter. I told you, even when the truth came out, I wasn't going back on that promise. From everything I can tell, Luke is a good man, and he loves her. Our daughter is quite blessed to have so many people in her life who care about her."

Once again, Maddie was thankful she had called off her wedding to Brady before they'd hurt each other even more. Having him as a friend was a huge blessing in her life that she thanked God for daily.

"How is Josie doing?" Maddie asked, changing the subject to give Brady some breathing room.

Brady shook his head. "Not feeling great, but Laura took Shana for the day so Josie could rest."

Maddie would've never imagined having such a deep love for the woman who had once been her childhood nemesis. But the concern on Brady's face also brought the same feeling to Maddie's heart.

"Let me know if there's anything I can do," Maddie said.

Brady nodded. "People have been bringing us

meals and helping Josie with Shana, so we just need to wait for the morning sickness to pass." Then Brady chuckled. "Whoever called that morning sickness sure doesn't know how long the morning is supposed to last."

Maddie had always considered herself fortunate that she had a relatively easy pregnancy with Kayla. Her heart warmed as she remembered that was one of the questions Luke had been concerned about. Even though she'd had Brady, Luke had been very worried that he hadn't been there to help her during that time.

Just one more reason why Maddie couldn't help liking him.

Brady walked over to Luke and Granny. "Luke." He held his hand out to the other man, and Luke took it. Brady always made the extra effort to make Luke feel comfortable, and it made her happy to see the men getting along. They both understood that the most important person in this equation was Kayla, and no matter how many times Maddie saw this interaction, she would never cease to be grateful.

Maddie joined the group, greeting Luke and Granny. But when she gave Granny a hug, Granny seemed to cling a little tighter than usual.

"I've missed you," Granny said.

"I check in on you every night when I come to work," Maddie said.

Maddie's new shift didn't start until after visiting hours were over, and one of the aides always made sure that Briana's car wasn't in the parking lot.

"I know, I know," Granny said. "But I'm usually asleep by the time you're done with your report, so I never get to see you."

Maddie smiled. "I always leave you a little something so you know I've been by."

Maddie had talked to the dietitian, who'd found some sugar-free chocolate that Granny could have in moderation. It wasn't much, but every night, Maddie left one at Granny's bedside.

Granny gave half a smile. "Just to mess with her, I told Briana those chocolates were from my boyfriend."

Luke laughed. "It has been pretty funny watching Briana try to figure out who Granny's boyfriend is and whether or not he's after her money."

Kayla laughed with them. "I even brought flowers one day, and we told her it was from her boyfriend."

Maddie laughed as she shook her head. "You shouldn't tell tales like that."

"And Briana shouldn't be causing so much trouble," Granny said. "I have a mind to take her out of my will if she doesn't start behaving."

"No," they all said together, then laughed.

Maddie looked at Granny. "Given that Briana

is already afraid you're being taken advantage of financially, that would be a terrible thing to do."

Granny straightened. "And it would serve her right since she cares more about my money than my happiness." Then she smiled over at Luke and Kayla. "And it's been a long time since I've been this happy. Not since my Gerald died."

Her eyes got misty, as they always did when she talked about her late husband. Then she looked from Maddie to Luke and back at Maddie again. "You know, the greatest gift I've ever had in my life was the love of my Gerald. You two had something once, so maybe you should find out if there's still a spark."

Maddie tried not to groan. "No offense to Luke, but my romance days are over. I've made so many mistakes, and I'm not willing to make a mistake with Kayla's father. I wouldn't do anything to hurt our relationship."

Granny stared at her. "Well, it seems to me you've already gone and made one big mistake." Then her voice softened. "But you know, we shouldn't allow our mistakes to control us. We all have made mistakes. What matters is not the mistakes you make, but getting up and trying again. Don't give up on love just because it's never worked out for you."

Maddie had been given that advice before, and it wasn't that she disagreed, but given all her mistakes, sometimes she thought that it was her punishment for all the people she hurt in her life. Maybe she didn't deserve that kind of love.

Luke caught her eye, as if to say he understood what she meant and where she was coming from. "No offense taken," he said. "Granny, you know I love you, but I'm with Maddie on this one. My focus right now is building a relationship with my daughter, not trying to do a romantic reconciliation of my past. Like Maddie, I've made more than my share of mistakes, including how I treated her back then. Right now, what Maddie and I both need is to be friends so that we can learn how to be good co-parents to our daughter and not let all that other stuff interfere."

While Maddie was grateful to be on the same page as Luke, she felt a small pang of regret at his "just friends" comment. It wasn't that he was wrong, but a tiny part of her did wish for something more. When she said that she'd made so many mistakes dating, she had been telling the truth. But she hadn't met anyone with Luke's character, either.

"I need to go finish getting my horse ready," Kayla said. "You guys can sit in the stands and wait."

Then she grinned, smiling over at Granny before looking back at them. "Mom and Dad, you should sit together."

It was obvious what she was trying to do, and Brady, bless him, grinned. "That is such a great idea," he said. "I'm glad I don't need to be in the arena today. I get to watch. It will be nice sitting and talking to your mom about your riding."

Kayla scowled. "That's not who I meant, Dad, and you know it. But maybe I need to come up with different nicknames for you guys so that when I say 'Dad,' you know which one of you I'm talking about."

With that, she turned and headed back toward where the horses were kept. Brady clapped Luke on the back. "I do need to go supervise, and I'd like to say that we raised her better than that. But the truth is that she is exactly what we raised her to be. A strong woman who knows her mind and isn't afraid to speak it. It can be annoying parenting her sometimes, but I think it will serve her well as she goes out into the world."

"I agree," Luke said. "So many kids I see these days act entitled, so I think the two of you have done a fine job turning our daughter into an exceptional young woman."

It was strange seeing the genuine way these men complemented each other. Although Maddie believed in the idea of confessing her sins and obtaining forgiveness, sometimes it was hard to reconcile that idea with the fact that she couldn't entirely regret her actions. Her sins had led to her daughter having these two great fathers. Maddie would have never been able to raise Kayla so well on her own, and it was weird living in that tension. The only thing she could cling to was God and the fact that things intended for harm could be used to glorify God. She had to believe that's what happened here.

Though Maddie wanted to sit as far away as possible from Luke just to spite her daughter, given that this was the first time Luke had gotten to see Kayla ride, Maddie wanted to be near him to explain everything. Or at least that's what she told herself. She would be lying if she said that she didn't breathe in Luke's cologne a little more deeply than was proper. She tried telling herself that it wasn't her fault he smelled like the air after a summer's rain.

When Kayla and the other riders entered the arena, Granny immediately pointed her out. "There she is," Granny said, sounding excited.

Granny's happiness made Maddie glad they had told her the truth as soon as possible. Granny's joy at seeing Kayla brought renewed attention and regret to Maddie that Granny had been denied this experience for so long.

Luke reached over and took Maddie's hand. "Don't do that to yourself," he said.

Maddie looked over at him. "What?"

He shrugged. "The regret. I know that look in

your eyes. It's the same one that haunted me for so long and kept me from coming home. You can blame yourself all you want, but the truth is, we both made mistakes. And I haven't seen you hating on me the way you hate on yourself over it."

Wow. How did he know all that about her? She wanted to ask, but then she noticed that Granny was looking over at them with a twinkle in her eye, which meant she had seen him take her hand. Maddie quickly pulled her hand away and shoved her hands in her pockets.

"I saw that," Granny said. "You don't have to hide your feelings from me."

Luke glanced at Granny and rolled his eyes. "Stop. We've already told you that our focus is on Kayla, not each other. You keep up your antics, and I'm going to make you go to Drake's birthday party tomorrow by yourself."

The look of horror on Granny's face made Maddie laugh. "You wouldn't."

Though there was a twinkle in Luke's eyes, he said, "Oh, I would. Just think. You, stuck at Briana's house all day, all by yourself, with no one to protect you from her incessant nagging."

"At least there will be decent food," Granny grumbled as they all laughed.

Then Luke said, "Come on, you know I wouldn't really do that to you. You asked me to go with you, and I said I would, so I am. I even got Drake a present."

Granny relaxed slightly, and Luke added, "I mean it, though. You stay out of my business. We do not want or need your help with our love life."

"Fine," Granny said. "But I'd like to point out that the two of you aren't getting any younger, and you're still young enough to give me more great-grandchildren, so hurry up."

Ouch. Granny was pushing the timeline on things, and the thought unsettled her. Something stirred within her as she imagined doing it all over again with Luke, raising their child together. Luke could experience all the things he missed with Kayla. But she quickly realized those thoughts were inappropriate.

Besides, jumping into something too soon was what had gotten her into this mess. If anything were to happen romantically for Maddie, it would take time, consideration, and careful thought. She'd have to be even more cautious with Luke, given that if anything happened between them and it didn't work out, the person who'd be the most hurt was Kayla.

But as Luke adjusted the collar on Granny's coat and she saw the tender way they looked at each other, Maddie was reminded that if she were to pursue a romantic relationship, Luke was the kind of man she would want to date.

* * *

What had Granny been thinking, making such an insensitive comment about babies? Luke could see the uncomfortable look on Maddie's face, just as he noticed all the ways she'd reacted to everything else today.

He tried keeping his eyes on his daughter as she was riding around the edge of the arena, but it was hard to pay attention when his thoughts kept drifting to Maddie.

"They're just warming up the horses right now," Maddie said, leaning over him and toward Granny.

The brush of her sleeve against his was accidental, but it reminded him of how briefly he held her hand, and that he liked her touch. He thought he'd given her some comfort, too, at least until Granny ruined it.

But how was he supposed to fault her? He knew that all of Granny's remarks came from a place of love. She wanted to see them both happy, and even before Luke and Maddie had officially met, Granny had long been telling him about the nice woman in the senior center that she thought would be a good match for him. He now knew she'd been talking about Maddie. He'd always shrugged off her suggestion, but obviously, Granny knew something they didn't.

Kayla rode over to the edge of the arena. "I'm

going to be leading today," she said, a wide grin on her face.

"That's great," Maddie said. "It'll be easy for everyone to spot you."

Maddie gave a wave, and then Kayla turned and rode off, lining up her horse with the other horses in the arena.

Maddie turned to them. "What Kayla is doing today is called a drill. Basically, they ride the horses in different formations to make patterns in time with the music. It's quite beautiful to watch, but it requires a lot of talent and precision on the part of the riders to make sure that everyone is in the right place in the arena at the right time, or someone could get seriously hurt."

Granny snorted. "It's not as if I haven't been watching drills for most of my life. I know what she's doing. And it's great that she gets to lead."

Maddie laughed. "I know, but I wasn't sure what Luke knew."

Luke turned to Maddie and smiled, appreciative that she took the time to include him. "Not much," he admitted. "I can ride, and I love being around horses, but this is a foreign world to me."

When he was a kid, summers with Briana here had been some of his favorite times. He was a city boy, and the country life was completely new and different to him. Sometimes he wished he could travel back to that one summer and make things right between Maddie and him, as well as fix Briana's view of him. But like he'd said to Maddie, there was no sense dwelling on what could have been. They had to accept the situation they were in now and make the most of it going forward.

Trying to ignore the warmth of the woman next to him, Luke focused his attention on the arena, where they had begun the drill.

After a few minutes, Granny clapped her hands, then gestured. "They're setting themselves up for a pass-through, aren't they?"

He glanced at Maddie to see the smile on her face. "They sure are. It's one of my favorite maneuvers." She pointed at the arena and said to Luke, "Horses don't naturally like to charge toward one another, so it takes a lot of skill and talent to get the horses to run toward each other and sustain momentum as they pass. It also requires a great deal of precision in their spacing so that no one crashes into each other."

Luke held his breath as he watched his daughter and her horse charge in their group toward another group of riders and horses. Sure enough, they passed right through each other, ending up on the other side.

"That was spectacular," Luke said. "My heart skipped a beat there for a second. You must be a nervous wreck watching her sometimes."

Even though Granny's scrutiny earlier had made them uncomfortable, Maddie took his hand and gave it a squeeze before letting it go. "And to think you haven't seen her ride trick. I'm pretty sure every single one of these premature grays on my head is from her."

A soft smile filled her face, and it was hard not to remark on how beautiful she looked in that moment.

"But just look at her. Look at that grin. Kayla loves what she's doing, and even though I get nervous, having done it myself, I know that she's got the necessary skills, as well as instructors who are focused on her safety at all times."

He'd forgotten that Maddie had been a trick rider herself. "That's right," he said. "I remember you talking about that the night we met. You were so mad about someone named Junior taking your spot."

Maddie groaned. "Thanks for that reminder. I was such a mess back then. I hated Junior because I thought she had everything handed to her, and she was taking what I deserved."

A dark look crossed Maddie's face, and Luke wanted to reach out to her again as she wrestled with one more regret from her past.

"Junior goes by Josie now," Maddie continued. "You might remember her as Brady's wife. I did a lot of horrible things, but thankfully, God gave us another chance, and now she is one of my dearest friends."

Luke nodded slowly, realizing just what an amazing environment Kayla had grown up in. He was glad his daughter had been raised with such love and Christlike examples. He knew that if he said that to Maddie, she would argue with him, but what he was learning about the love of God was that no one was perfect all the time, but was loved just the same. And that love was what helped other people to emulate that same behavior. Even though they wanted to be like God, they couldn't do it right all the time, and that was okay.

Instead, he said, "Yeah, well, just remember, I wasn't much of a prince then either. But I was just thinking how grateful I am that God can still redeem us for mistakes. It's really neat that you and Josie were able to become friends."

He was rewarded with another beautiful smile. "Funny, I had the same train of thought earlier. In spite of everything I've done wrong, God has chosen to bless us richly."

"Maybe someday we can find that kind of forgiveness with Briana," Luke said.

"That harpy?" Granny asked. "She's always been a spoiled petulant child."

Luke shook his head. "That's not true. She was one of my best friends when we were kids. I had so much fun the summers I came out to visit. Earlier, I was thinking how much I wished we could somehow regain that relationship."

Granny snorted. "That was before she discovered popularity and all that nonsense. These days, all Briana cares about is what other people think. Her house has to be perfect, she has to drive the nicest car, go to the salon all the time, and everything else she thinks will make people notice her. I find it nauseating. She wasn't raised that way."

A weird pang of sympathy hit Luke's heart. "Does it matter? Granted, I've just recently come back to Christ and the church, but Jesus loves her, too."

Even with the horses going at full speed in front of them, Granny's indrawn breath could clearly be heard.

"I suppose you're right," she said. "I haven't been much of a Christian to her lately because she's been so annoying."

Luke looked at Granny's hand and gave it the same comforting squeeze he'd given Maddie. "We both know that the Bible doesn't say love one another except for when the other person is being annoying. I also know it's hard, and I haven't done a very good job either, so why don't we all just resolve to do better? Sure, we won't be perfect, but we should at least try."

The tears forming in Granny's eyes made it hard for Luke to get those last words out. "God surely did give me the greatest gift when we brought you home," she said.

If he spoke now, he was liable to say something stupid, mostly because his head was filled with so many regrets and wishes for having done better, despite all of his earlier thoughts that it was pointless to do so. Instead, he sat in silence with the others as they continued watching Kayla ride the drill.

He had to agree with Maddie. Their daughter was magnificent. Her wide smile and bright eyes told him that she was in her happy place.

When the ride was over, Luke started to help Granny out of her seat, but she was already pushing him away, and in doing so, she started to lose her balance. He grabbed her by the wrist to keep her from falling all the way down, but she still banged her knee on the side of the bleachers.

"Granny, are you okay?" Maddie asked.

"Get your paws off me," Granny said. "I'm fine. I just stumbled a bit, and suddenly everyone's acting like the world is ending."

"It's only because we care," Luke said. "Besides, if you want to be home again, the last thing we need is for you to fall and break your hip even worse."

He got her walker situated and set it in front of her. "Now, no complaints about the walker this time, you hear?"

Granny mumbled something under her breath that he couldn't hear, but he knew she was frustrated that he was right. They made their way out of the stands, and Maddie directed them through a large lobby and into another area where the horses were kept.

"Kayla will be a few minutes getting her horse unsaddled, so I thought I would show you around. I know Granny is already familiar with everything, but Luke might want to see where Kayla spends most of her time."

Walking through the stables, Luke was reminded of visiting his grandparents as a child. Obviously, it was nothing elaborate like Shepherd's Creek, but the smell of hay and animals brought him back. Granny paused at one of the stalls.

"That looks just like Caramello, the first horse your grandfather bought me," Granny said.

Maddie paused at the stall and turned to them. "That's Stolley Bear, and if I remember correctly, Shepherd's Creek bought a bunch of horses from you and your husband back when you were breeding. It's possible he might come from that stock."

Granny's eyes filled with tears, and her voice quivered as she said, "Wouldn't that be something? You sell off your horses, but you never know what ends up happening to them. I'm pretty sure Gerald did sell some to Big Joe, but like you, I would have to look at the records to be sure."

Even though she wasn't close enough to touch Stolley Bear, Granny reached her hand toward him.

Maddie held her arm out to Granny. "Let me move you closer so you can pet him. He's one of the sweetest horses you'll ever meet."

Luke watched with gratitude as Maddie helped Granny get closer to the horse. Stolley Bear lowered his head as if he knew Granny wanted to pet him, and Granny gently stroked the horse's nose.

The simple gesture made his grandmother so happy, and Luke loved the way Maddie gave such care and attention to Granny, helping her with the horse, and also giving her a steadying hand that didn't seem to bother Granny. The rich brown of the horse did indeed look like caramel.

Granny sighed a couple of times, saying, "Ah, Caramello."

He didn't know how long she stood there, petting the horse. The look of gratitude he gave Maddie was a silent acknowledgment that he appreciated she wasn't rushing them through or pushing them to the next activity.

He had intentionally kept the day free so they could all do whatever they wanted.

Before long, Kayla came bounding over. "What did you think of my ride?" she asked.

Granny never took her eyes off Stolley Bear but said, "It was wonderful. Did you know that this horse looks just like a horse I once had, Caramello?"

Just like her mother, Kayla smiled indulgently. "Oh, that's great. Maybe you could find a picture of her or something, and we can compare."

Granny nodded. "As soon as I get out of that death trap they have me locked up in."

Maddie shook her head. "It's not a death trap. The senior center has one of the highest quality and safety ratings in the state. It's so highly rated that we have people from all over trying to get in."

Granny turned and scowled at Maddie. "They can have my spot. Why can't I just go home when I have Luke able to stay there and take care of me?"

Luke watched the exasperated expression flit across Maddie's face before she smiled and said, "We've already been through this. Your doctor hasn't cleared you to do so. But keep working on your physical therapy exercises and following all of your other instructions, and I promise, you'll be home before you know it."

He appreciated that she didn't mention he hadn't completed the necessary renovations to Granny's house. It seemed like every simple project had turned into a bigger project. When he peeled back the carpet to fix one broken step, he'd realized the entire staircase needed replacing.

As frustrating as it was for Granny to have to wait, he wanted her house to be safe so she wouldn't have any more falls or other injuries that would prevent her from living at home permanently.

Maddie held her hand out to Granny. "How about we go get some lunch now, and we'll walk by Brady's office and see if he can look up any information on Stolley Bear's parentage?"

Though Granny looked reluctant, she nodded. "As long as you're not going to make me eat that health garbage."

Maddie laughed. "Actually, since you're missing pizza day at the senior center, I was thinking we could go out for pizza."

Granny's eyes widened. "Pizza? Like from Giorgio's?"

Maddie grinned. "Is there any other pizza place in town?"

"Mom and I always go to Giorgio's on Saturdays for lunch. It's our thing," Kayla said, smiling at her mom.

Luke didn't know why, but tears stung the back of his eyes at the thought. He was being included in their family traditions. Sure, they had made it clear that he was part of the family, but something about being included in their routine solidified his place with them. As they walked back to the stables, Granny kept turning backward to look at Stolley Bear.

"On your next visit, we can allow for some extra time for you to get to know him better," Kayla offered. "And even help you ride him. Stolley Bear is gentle enough that we often use him for some of the other seniors as well as small children and people with disabilities."

While Granny's face lit up, Maddie shook her head. "That won't be for a while. We need to check with her doctor to make sure she is healed properly and he thinks it's safe. They're working hard to get Granny off her walker, so maybe we can use this as incentive for her to actually do her physical therapy exercises instead of spending half of her session complaining at her therapist."

Granny scowled, but then she said, "Really? You'll let me ride?"

Maddie nodded. "You know I am a big believer in people being as active as they can be. It's what keeps us young, healthy, and vibrant. But like I said, we need your doctor's approval first. Where you're at in your physical therapy, he is not going to give it. So, do we have a deal? Are you going to give your all in physical therapy so that you can get well enough to ride the horse?"

Even though Luke felt like they'd been having the conversation over and over about Granny's desire to go home, the expression on her face told him that this might just be the ticket. He loved the way Maddie was always creative about how she dealt with Granny. So many times, he saw how Briana just forced issues and bossed Granny around. Then Granny would get cranky because she didn't like having someone tell her what to do.

Once again, Luke was grateful that Granny had Maddie in her life. Even though Maddie had been moved to the night shift, when Luke visited Granny during the day, he noticed how so many of Granny's friends often threw something about what Maddie said or did into the conversation. She was well-loved by the residents, and Luke could see why.

Moments like these made it hard for Luke to resist Granny's matchmaking efforts. Maddie was everything he could want in a woman, and more, but not only had she made it clear she wasn't interested in being anything more than friends, she was right to say so.

Chapter Five

Having to come in early for her Sunday evening shift was never a good sign, especially if it was her boss texting her to report directly to her office when she got there. When Maddie showed up in Claire's office, Claire looked like she wanted to rip her hair out, except that Briana was standing next to her, fuming, and Luke looked about ready to cry.

"What's going on here?" Maddie asked.

"I want you fired, that's what's going on," Briana said. "And I'm filing charges of elder abuse against Luke. The police are on their way."

Looking exasperated, Claire said, "The police are not on their way. The doctor is examining Ida Mae now, and the social worker is there as well. They will decide whether or not the police are necessary."

Instead of being happy that Granny was getting the best of care, the bright red shade of Briana's face only intensified. "She'll just lie to protect them. Granny is so happy to have Luke home and a so-called new granddaughter that she's going to lie to hide the truth. She's always wanted more great-grandchildren, so she's going to do whatever it takes to not risk it. I'm still not convinced that Kayla is Luke's."

Luke glared at his cousin. "I have all the proof I need, but just so people like you will shut up, we took a paternity test, and the results are being processed. But regardless, it's none of your business, so you need to let it go."

"I'm not letting it go," Briana said. "You are taking advantage of an old woman, and I won't allow it to happen."

Because Maddie knew she was already on thin ice, she remained silent at the cousins' bickering choosing to take a wait and see approach, since she'd find out the details soon enough. She wanted to tell Briana that it was ridiculous the way she was standing in the way of an old woman's happiness, and if she really wanted what was best for Granny, she would do what she could to be a partner in the situation and not an adversary.

"That's part of why the social worker is there," Claire said. "Given that we have two family members fighting over the situation with Ida Mae, Eva will not only check on these abuse allegations, but she will also be looking out for Ida Mae to make sure that her best interests are being taken care of. I know both of you are coming from a place of caring about Ida Mae, but since you can't agree, Eva will be a neutral party to make sure that we are serving Ida Mae's best interests."

Even though having to bring in a social worker meant paperwork and hassle, in this case, Maddie was grateful they had the option. While Maddie was certain that Eva wouldn't find any evidence of abuse, it would be reassuring to all parties to know that Granny was getting the best care possible.

"And what about Maddie?" Briana demanded. "I gave specific instructions that she was to have no contact with Granny, and yet that direction was ignored."

Claire pressed her fingers to her temples. Maddie felt sorry for the woman, who had been brought in on her day off to deal with this nonsense.

"As I have explained to you, Maddie is a trusted employee who has done nothing wrong. Given that we're in a small town where everyone knows each other, there's no way we can dictate who talks to who outside of the center. I can't dictate what Maddie does during her time off. Luke took your grandmother on an outing as approved by her doctor, and I have no control over whether or not they see Maddie there."

While Claire had explained all this before, it still felt to Maddie like she was being punished.

But as Claire had privately told Maddie, they needed to do whatever they could to keep negative attention off Maddie while they were searching for Claire's replacement.

"You still haven't addressed Maddie's involvement," Briana screeched. "Is she responsible for those bruises that I saw on Granny? I have a hard time believing that Granny simply stumbled."

Bruises? Maddie looked at Luke and then over at Claire. "What's this about Granny having bruises? Clearly, I'm missing something."

Claire's face remained stoic. "Earlier today at her son's birthday party, Briana noticed that Ida Mae had a limp and some bruising on her arm. Though Ida Mae said it was an accident that happened while at Shepherd's Creek Stables, we are doing our due diligence to make sure."

At first, Maddie was confused, because there had been no accident. Then she remembered. "Wait, you mean when she had a hard time getting out of her seat in the stands? I was there. She started to fall, and Luke tried to help her, but she didn't want help."

Claire looked at her notes and wrote something down. "That's what I have been told," Claire said. "But that's also why we have Ida Mae alone with the doctor and the social worker, to make sure."

By the tension in Claire's voice, Maddie knew Claire thought this whole thing was ridiculous.

But because they took every accusation of elder abuse seriously, they would have to do a full investigation. It hadn't occurred to Maddie that Granny would have any bruising or even a limp afterward, but she'd forgotten how delicate the elderly woman's skin could be, so it was possible that there might be some bruising.

"I'm sure they got together and concocted a story," Briana said.

"And as I told you," Claire said, "our doctors and social workers are trained to look for signs of abuse as well as signs that the abused party is lying to protect their abuser. I realize that this is new to you, but our team is very experienced in investigating elder abuse. Please let everyone do their jobs, and I promise, everything will be done to make sure that Ida Mae is safe. Her needs are the most important thing here."

Were Maddie not under suspicion, she would go and grab some chocolate out of the hidden stash in her desk to make Claire feel better. But Briana would likely use it against her in some way. Briana wasn't the first overbearing family member that Maddie had to deal with, far from it. But it had never hit home so personally before.

A knock sounded at the door, and Dr. Reynolds came in. "I've finished examining Ida Mae, and everything's fine. The bruise looks much worse than it actually is. She's limping because she's been neglecting her physical therapy exercises, and she overexerted herself. She just needs to stay on top of her physical therapy, regain her strength, and I'm fully convinced that she'll be running laps around us in no time."

Briana looked over at the doctor, a disdainful expression on her face. "But you admit they pushed her beyond her limits. I think we need some very strong boundaries about Granny's physical limitations, and they shouldn't be taking her to such an unsafe place as horse stables."

The doctor gave her a firm but compassionate look. "I disagree," he said. "The only reason I said Ida Mae overexerted herself is that she hasn't been doing her exercises. The truth is, someone in her stage of recovery should be able to participate in all of that without feeling adverse effects. I'm hoping this is the wake-up call she needs to realize that her exercises are for her own good."

Then he looked over at Luke. "As for taking her to the stables, I think it's good for her to be out in the fresh air. She loves animals, and this is a great way to get her interacting with them. More importantly, it's a reminder of the life she misses, and motivation to get her on the road to recovery. Most of what's wrong with your grandmother isn't about her injury, but about her attitude and motivation to get well. I think you might've hit on just the thing she needs."

"But she got hurt," Briana said.

Dr. Reynolds shrugged. "When you have a small child, do you keep them from playing on the playground because of a skinned knee? That's really what we're talking about here, or at least the same principle. While I would like for Luke to talk to her physical therapist about additional ways to help Ida Mae, both in keeping her safe and helping her push her limits in safe ways, I think more outings just like this are exactly what she needs."

Though in many ways, this was a victory for Luke, he still looked dejected. Maddie wished she could give him a hug or even squeeze his hand or something. That was the trouble with having such blurred lines between personal and professional life. Anything she did that seemed to be in support of Luke, especially in front of Briana, would only set Briana off and give credence to her accusations of bias. As it was, not only was Maddie's job on thin ice, but everything she had worked for professionally was so close to falling apart.

"Thank you, Dr. Reynolds," Claire said. "I believe you've put all of our minds at ease."

The doctor nodded. "Of course. As I said, I hope this motivates her to take her recovery seriously."

Claire made another note in her file, then

looked up at them. "You both can go see Ida Mae now," she said. "The social worker will be in touch with each of you to set up an appointment to talk about your individual concerns. You'll both have a chance to speak with her, and the social worker will investigate."

"And what about Maddie?" Briana asked.

Claire closed her file and stood up. "We have zero evidence that Maddie has done anything wrong. Though we did switch her shift to accommodate you, you have to remember that your grandmother is not our only patient. There will be times when Maddie is needed to take care of her, and I have full confidence in her ability to do so."

Then Claire looked over at Luke. "If Luke wishes to interact with Maddie outside of the nursing home while your grandmother is present, there is nothing wrong with that. Unless you have real evidence, I will no longer entertain your complaints against one of my best employees."

Tears welled up in Maddie's eyes at Claire's defense. All this time, she'd been afraid of losing her job, but it was clear that Claire firmly had her back.

"Fine," Briana said. "But I will be watching. There is nothing more important to me than my grandmother's safety and health. So do not think that you can lull me into complacency simply because you can't do your job."

Without waiting for a response, Briana got up and walked out of the office. Luke remained seated, still looking worried.

"Give it to me straight," he said quietly. "I love Granny, and I truly do want what's best for her. How do I handle this and protect my grandmother?"

It was the right question to ask. Judging from the sympathetic look on Claire's face, she thought so, too. "Just keep doing what you're doing. I know Briana is upset, but Ida Mae is happier and making progress, so I have to believe that you are having a positive effect. Of course, the social worker will make the final decision, but as long as you are following the instructions of her doctors and caregivers, you are doing all the right things."

Luke nodded slowly. "Okay," he said. "But please know, I'm willing to do whatever it takes to help my grandmother."

Maddie wished she could reach out to him and tell him how much she admired him. Although Claire had stuck up for her, Maddie still needed to be careful about what she said and did at the Senior Center.

When Luke left, Maddie turned to Claire. "What are we supposed to do about Briana? I'm trying to do the right thing, but it's hard when she wants to have me fired."

Claire shook her head. "Honestly, I don't know. This is all new territory for me. I believe in you and your integrity, and I know that everything Briana is saying is false. But as the director of the center, you know I have to do my due diligence."

Maddie nodded. "I know. It just seems so unfair, the way Briana is attacking us, and no one's done anything wrong."

Claire nodded. "I agree. But we promised our residents that we would do our best for them, so here we are. Honestly, I'm glad that Briana made an official allegation of abuse because that means the social worker who has been brought in will do a thorough investigation, clearing both you and Luke of all wrongdoing. Once that happens, she can't complain anymore. And hopefully, then Ida Mae will return to her own house, and we can all get back to business. Briana won't like it, but I think Ida Mae will be happier, and it will be easier on everyone."

As Maddie turned to leave, Claire added, "That said, we do need to talk about your involvement with Luke."

Maddie froze with her hand on the doorknob. "What do you mean?"

A compassionate look filled Claire's face. "I know you two share a child, so you have to interact. But a person would have to be blind to miss the fact that you and Luke have chemistry.

There's nothing in the employee handbook prohibiting a romance between the two of you, but I'm thinking of the optics here. Briana has a big mouth, and while I can disprove her allegations about Ida Mae, don't give her a reason to start rumors about you and Luke."

Closing her eyes briefly, Maddie took a deep breath. "We're just friends."

"With chemistry," Claire said. "Look, I'm on your side, and personally, I would be thrilled for you to finally meet Mr. Right. But Briana is out to get you, and if she can't get you fired for mistreating Ida Mae, she'll find some other way to hurt you."

Maddie hated that Claire was right. Not about the chemistry part, though. "Like I said, we're just friends."

"Fine." Claire gave her an exasperated look. "Just watch your back. And don't do anything with Luke that she can twist into making you look bad."

Well, it was too late for that, since Maddie had already had a child with him, but she got Claire's point.

"Okay," Maddie said. "Message received."

Claire sighed. "I didn't mean it like that. I know I'm your boss, but I'm speaking as a friend who wants to see you succeed. You've worked so hard to get where you're at. I don't want someone like Briana ruining it for you. In a few months, this will all be over, and then you and Luke can pursue whatever it is between you."

Even though Maddie knew Claire was trying to encourage her, it didn't help to have one more person pointing out things between her and Luke. "Luke and I are clear on the fact that we're just friends. We won't be pursuing anything, now, or in a few months."

Though Maddie spoke with conviction, her heart hurt at the words. Claire was right that Maddie had worked hard to get where she was at, not just with her career, but in being seen as a respectable part of society after everything she'd been through. If her reputation could be ruined so easily by Briana's accusations, then had Maddie really accomplished anything?

"Thanks for the support," Maddie said, opening the door. "I'll do my best to make sure I'm not upsetting Briana in any way."

And make sure people stopped talking about Maddie and Luke. Since Maddie hadn't done anything wrong in her interaction with him, there was only one solution: to avoid him as much as possible.

Luke watched with pride as Granny took a few steps without her walker in her physical therapy session. Ever since their visit to the stables a couple weeks ago, Granny had become more determined to take her physical therapy seriously and was focused on going home. Even though the social worker had said it wasn't necessary, Luke was doing everything in his power to ensure that he was an active participant in Granny's care and that everyone knew he was there for her. There was nothing more important in his life than taking care of Granny and helping her come home.

His phone beeped with an incoming text message, and when he opened it, Luke smiled. Kayla was the other reason he was doing everything he could for his family. He would have never imagined just how much becoming a father would mean to him, and he was so grateful for this chance to be in her life. Kayla had made arrangements for an extra practice today, and wanted to know if he and Granny could come along. That was more than he had expected: just how much his daughter and the rest of her family wanted him to be part of her life.

When Granny and her physical therapist stopped for a brief rest, Luke asked, "Kayla invited us to go see her ride again today. Do you want to go?"

They'd been back to the stables a few times now, so he knew Granny would be excited at the opportunity. For him, that was an even bigger joy: seeing Granny so happy. As much as he had hated the feeling of letting her down by not accepting responsibility for his actions all those years ago, it was clear that Granny was taking this in stride. If you asked him, Kayla was also a huge reason for all the progress Granny was making.

"Of course I do," Granny said. "One of these days, I'm going to get back on a horse."

The physical therapist chuckled as she shook her head. "Keep up with your exercises, and I think you'll be able to do it eventually."

Luke had seen a lot of beautiful things in his time, but the way Granny's face lit up at the physical therapist's encouragement had to be one of the most dazzling sights he'd ever seen. Back in the day, his grandmother had been one of the beauties of the area, and when she smiled like that, he could see why. Sometimes he thought he saw a bit of Granny in his daughter, and he liked the idea of having been able to pass down something so remarkable.

He responded to Kayla's text, then observed as Granny finished up her routine. After which, Luke escorted his grandmother back to her room to get ready for the outing. Before they left, he paused at the nurses' station to give them an update on the plan. Even though he knew it wasn't yet time for Maddie's shift, Luke glanced around wistfully, hoping to get a glimpse of her. Sometimes she came in early for meetings, and even though she'd told him that for professional reasons, she had to keep her distance from both him and Granny at the senior center, he couldn't help looking.

"She's got the night off," the nurse at the station said.

"Who?" he asked, trying to sound innocent. Maddie had asked him to not add fuel to the fire when it came to people's interest in their relationship, so hopefully this would throw them off the scent. It seemed like everywhere he went, Briana had spies, and the last thing he needed was for someone to gossip about him to her.

The nurse grinned. "We're not blind, you know. You like Maddie. She likes you. It's really a shame that Briana is so difficult."

Luke didn't want to agree with her, just in case. "It's not like that," he said. "We share a child, so of course we care about each other. We want the best for our daughter."

The nurse nodded. "You can say that, but it's obvious to everyone. Mark my words, this time next year, you two will be married."

Before he could answer, the nurse walked over to the board where they kept notes about their patients and made a note about Granny leaving with him. Maddie had told them that they usually didn't make such a big deal of all of this, but with Briana's accusations, they over-documented everything, just in case.

He'd get to see Maddie without the prying eyes of the staff, and his steps felt a little lighter as he headed back to make sure that Granny was ready to go.

When he got to Granny's room, Briana was sitting in Briana's usual spot.

"Granny says you're taking her to the stables again," Briana said.

Luke pasted a smile on his face. "Yes. We go to all of Kayla's practices. We've both missed out on so much of her life that we don't want to miss a second more."

Briana glared at him. "My son has a band concert tonight."

Right. If it wasn't concern over Granny's health, it was some way that he was interfering with Briana's family.

"I know," he said. "I have it all planned out. We're going to watch Kayla ride, grab a quick dinner, and then we'll be at the school in time for the concert."

His reassuring words didn't erase the scowl off Briana's face. "You know Granny can't have fast food. I hope you don't make a habit of this."

"It's a good thing I have a healthy soup in the crockpot," he said, grinning. "I agree on fast food. I never liked it much. As soon as I learned about Granny's special diet, I got a list of recipes from the dietitian so I can make foods she can eat."

Briana looked down her nose at him. "You cook?"

Luke laughed as he patted his belly. "Do I look like I spent my life starving to death? I enjoy cooking, and it's always given me comfort, no matter where I am. When I remember the slop the military gave me to eat, it makes me all the more thankful that I can cook."

"And he's a good cook, too," Granny said. "Unlike in this place, healthy doesn't taste like garbage."

He shook his head at Granny. "I told you, it's all in the seasoning. They can't use these spices in the food here because there are too many dietary restrictions. But at home, we can add as many spices that are on the list as we like."

Briana still scowled, but he gestured at the little jar on Granny's dresser. "Hasn't the food here been better since I gave you your own set of spices to add to the food?"

He looked over at Briana and smiled, hoping to soften her a bit. "I really have to give you credit for doing such a good job taking care of her when she's so cranky. I know Granny isn't used to so many different spices, and she's turned up her nose at some of the names of things, but it's been really interesting to see how she has taken to the variety of new flavors."

Granny turned her attention to Briana. "I've even been eating that turmeric stuff that you told me was so good. I never liked the look or the sound of it, but Luke put it in some of my food, and I have to admit, it improved the flavor."

For once, Briana didn't look angry. She actually looked, dare he say, interested.

"Really? What did you make her?"

"It was one of those chicken recipes from the dietitian. I could see why Granny thinks the food is boring. If you add spices, turmeric being one of the primary ones, it can really enhance the flavor. If you like, I'll write it down for you."

Briana smiled. "That would be nice, thank you. Turmeric is one of my favorite spices."

Could his relationship with Briana finally be turning a corner?

This was the longest civil conversation he had had with Briana since coming back, and he saw a softness in her that made him realize how human she was. Maybe instead of fighting with her constantly, they could find ways like this to get along.

Granny banged her walker on the floor. "Can we finish playing Susie Homemaker and get on the road? I'd like to get to Kayla's ride early so I can get a good seat."

Luke grinned. Granny always said that, and she always sat in the same place. In all the times they had gone to the stables, no one was ever in that seat. But, getting there early meant he might have a few minutes to talk to Maddie.

They said goodbye to Briana and then headed out to the stables.

It was a beautiful spring day, and the sun was shining. The weather was warm enough that instead of wearing her sweater, Granny had put it in the little pouch in her walker. Some of the horses were out grazing, and a few were close to the fence.

"Can we go see the horses?" Granny asked.

"Of course," he said. "We've got plenty of time before Kayla's ride starts."

He had already glanced around the parking lot and hadn't seen signs of Maddie's truck yet. Maybe she'd join them by the horses. The more he got to know her, the more he realized that Maddie was a hard worker dedicated to her job and her daughter. She didn't often take a moment to pet the horses, so to speak. He admired that quality in her, but having led a similar life, dedicated to his job, not so much the family, he hoped she'd take advantage of his presence in Kayla's life to take some time for herself.

A lump formed in his throat at the thought of how seldom Maddie took a break. How long had Maddie been sacrificing her own personal happiness? Probably ever since Kayla came into the picture, and he hadn't been there to help her.

Sure enough, Maddie pulled in just as they got to the horses. He turned and waved at her, and she waved back. His heart did a tiny little somersault, and he felt like the teenage boy who'd seen her at that party and thought she was the prettiest girl there. Funny how some things never changed.

"I like that paint," Granny said, pointing to one of the horses. "Your grandfather and I used to look at them the way some people look to clouds, trying to find the patterns on their body and what they might be."

She gestured at a spot on the horse's back. "That one looks just like a hot dog," Granny said. "It's been ages since I've had a hot dog, but I've always loved them."

"And it will be ages until you get another one, if at all," Maddie said, coming up behind them. "They are terrible and contain way too much sodium. Your biggest problem right now is that you like too many salty and sweet things."

"A little salt never hurt anyone," Granny said, looking grumpy.

"I agree," Maddie said, smiling. "But too much salt is terrible for your heart and blood pressure."

He had to give Maddie credit. She really did try when it came to making sure that Granny's best interests were taken care of. He hoped that some of the things he was doing to help her would also be seen that way. Granny's insistence on salt being necessary to give food flavor was part of why he had begun his spice experiment with her. While it was true that you did need some salt in cooking, Granny had been the kind of person who would liberally dump salt from the saltshaker all over her food before even tasting it.

Now she was learning another way, and hopefully this would remain a good method for getting her to eat healthier.

"What's the name of the horse?" Granny asked, looking eager to change the subject.

Maddie stepped closer to the fence and held her hand out to the paint. "This guy is called Rascal," she said. "I've ridden him a time or two, and he lives up to his name."

Granny came closer and patted his neck. "That's real fine," she said. "A horse with a hot dog on his back has to be a rascal. I like him."

If Luke could pick the thing he loved the most about Maddie, it was the genuine way she smiled and her eyes lit up when Granny said something that amused her. She'd never taken on the patronizing attitude of so many others in the senior center who interacted with her. You could tell she genuinely liked Granny. That was how Maddie treated everyone—with the same kindness, dignity, and respect. No wonder she'd raised such a great daughter.

They spent a few minutes petting the horse. Then Maddie said, "We need to get moving. Kayla's ride starts in a few minutes."

It was probably for the best, considering he'd caught himself staring at Maddie and her beauty a little longer than was appropriate. Even though he intellectually knew that putting their daughter first and not getting caught up in all of this personal stuff was the right thing to do, his heart seemed to disagree, and he was constantly pulling it back in alignment with his mind.

But as he watched Maddie lean in and say something to Granny, Luke couldn't help wondering what it would be like to have Maddie as more than just his friend.

Chapter Six

Maddie was impressed with Luke for how quickly he had stepped up to be there for Kayla since finding out he was Kayla's father. He had come to every one of Kayla's practices, every school event, and whenever they invited him to something, he always said yes. Many of those times, Granny was with him. Maddie couldn't have asked for a better situation for their daughter.

The trouble was, the more time she spent with him, the more she found him attractive. It wasn't just the way he had gingerly helped Granny across the uneven ground, but it was the look of compassion and tenderness as he did so. Just as importantly, she saw the way he engaged with their daughter. He was genuinely interested in Kayla's activities, and it warmed her heart to see the way Kayla responded.

As they met Kayla at the stables, she was standing with Brady, probably going over today's practice. When Luke got to her, he asked her, "How was your day?"

Usually, if either she or Brady asked Kayla that question, Kayla would roll her eyes and tell them that it was fine. But Kayla, too, appeared to be trying, because she said, "It was great. And I didn't have to deal with Drake."

Both Luke and Brady laughed, but concern filled Maddie. She knew that tone in her daughter's voice, and it meant that Drake was picking on her. She hoped that Briana would have kept her feud to herself, but she supposed that was a bit too much to expect.

"Such an ill-mannered child," Granny said. "But I will give him credit. Ever since you came into the picture, he's been coming around more."

Granny snickered. "The spoiled brat is finally learning that he can't take me for granted. But I am sorry that he's not being nice to you. I just wish people understood that there is enough of everything to go around."

Maddie looked over at her daughter. "How bad is it?"

Kayla glanced over at Luke, and they exchanged a look before she shrugged. "Nothing I can't handle. Hopefully, as he gets used to the idea, things will be better. It's just harder because he never liked me anyway."

And that really was the trouble. Things might be different if Maddie and Briana had gotten along, and Kayla and Drake had gotten along.

But they'd been at odds for as long as Maddie could remember.

Kayla seemed to sense the direction of Maddie's thoughts. "Mom, it's fine. Like I said, nothing I can't handle. He is just being a jerk because he's jealous. I didn't do anything wrong. I'm not gonna let him make me feel bad for it. I love Granny, always have, and now that she's my actual Granny. I'm going to enjoy it, and no one can take that away from me."

She sent another look over to her father, and Maddie knew that the strength in her daughter had come from him. It kind of stung for Maddie. Kayla hadn't confided all this to her, and for a moment, she was a little bit envious. Which was silly, considering she had Kayla her whole life, and now it was Luke's turn to be there for their daughter. And it wasn't like Kayla was choosing sides or trying to make Maddie feel bad. She just had the opportunity to connect with her father on something important.

Kayla gave them all a quick hug, then dashed off to finish getting ready for her ride. This was another one of the sweet changes that had happened. Before Granny started coming to her practices, Maddie never got these few moments before practice. Kayla would be so busy with all her stuff, and if Maddie interrupted, she would get mad.

So even though it was hard, watching her daughter bond with someone else on such a deep level, she also had to be grateful because it was getting her a little time back as well.

As they walked into the stands, Luke put his hand on her arm. "I'm sorry if that felt like an intrusion," he said. "Kayla ran into him the other day at the nursing home, he made a couple of snide remarks about her, and I could tell it really upset her. So we spent a lot of time talking. I guess I should've told you about it."

There was so much sincerity in his voice that it was hard for her to feel bad. She could only feel grateful that he'd been there in that time of need.

"It's okay," she said. "I don't expect you to tell me everything. I just wish I'd known that he was giving her a hard time, that's all."

Luke nodded slowly. "I'm still learning how to do this parenting thing. You've got eighteen years on me, and I don't always know what to do. She made me promise not to tell you, but I guess that her saying that should have been my clue that it was something I should've told you."

Then he blew out a breath. "I just wanted her to trust me, you know? Like if she thought that I was going to you for everything, maybe she wouldn't tell me some stuff anymore. I guess I feel like I need to earn that trust by keeping her secrets."

The torment on his face made her feel even worse about the situation.

"No, it's fine. You're right. You should have your relationship with her. Kayla tells Brady a lot of things she doesn't share with me. But he ends up sharing most of it with me anyway. It's a delicate balance."

Luke nodded but looked confused. "Well, that was clear as mud," he said, shaking his head. "But you two had all this time to figure it out, so I imagine you probably messed things up a lot in the beginning."

Brady came up to them, cracking up. "In the beginning? We still mess things up. I got in trouble with Maddie the other day for giving Kayla some money. She asked for it because I didn't know Maddie had already told her no."

Even though Maddie had been really angry with Brady that day, she laughed with him. "We agreed that before either of us gives her money for anything, we talk about it. Otherwise, she'd play us all. She wanted a bunch of new clothes, and I told her she couldn't have any until she got rid of some of the stuff in her closet. Which she hasn't done, but she's now spending the money that you gave her to buy more clothes anyway."

Brady held his hands up like he was under arrest. "I know, and I'm sorry. Sometimes I just can't tell her no."

Then he put his hands down and looked over at Luke. "You see? We still don't have it figured out, but we do try to talk about it and work through whatever it is. Once I found out what Kayla did, I gave her a bunch of extra chores to pay me back."

Maddie shook her head. "But that doesn't change the fact that it looks like a bomb went off in her bedroom."

A guilty look crossed Luke's face. "Then I guess I should fess up that when we took Granny to the mall, I let Kayla buy a few things."

Then they all laughed, including Granny. "You see? They're all just a bunch of con artists," Granny said, chortling. Then she looked over at Maddie. "I did tell him that he should ask you before letting Kayla buy clothes. One of those shirts she picked out was scandalous."

They all laughed again. Kayla wasn't the sort to wear clothing that Maddie would consider scandalous, and she was dying to know what Granny thought was.

Maddie turned to Luke. "So, clearly we do need to have a conversation about this. At this point, I think we can all agree that Kayla does not need any new clothes. Except for a prom dress, and last year, she went shopping with her girlfriends and sent pictures to both me and Brady. We all decided together what we thought was appropriate. We'll just make sure she loops you in."

Another guilty look crossed Luke's face. "So I shouldn't have ordered her the one that she told me she really liked?"

Granny howled with laughter. "You all. This is more fun than making Briana think I have a boyfriend."

Brady groaned. "Well, we can only hope that it's not too ugly. I mean, she has modest taste, so it really can't be that bad. But the stuff that's in style right now is just awful."

Maddie appreciated the way Brady was taking this in stride. In truth, Brady was the one who cared the most about the kinds of dresses his daughter wore.

Maddie shrugged. "Well, she is eighteen, so I guess at some point we do have to let her grow up and make decisions for herself. But I hope this shows us all how important it is to communicate."

She looked over at Brady, who looked a little glum, but nodded. "I will add Luke to our group text. I guess we should've done it sooner."

All this time, Maddie had been feeling bad about how she felt her role had been taken over by Luke, but she couldn't imagine how Brady must feel, with another father in the picture.

Brady gestured at the stands. "You better get settled because we'll be starting in a few minutes."

He started walking to the entrance to the arena

so he could start instructing them, but Maddie ran to catch up with him.

"Thank you for what you did back there for Luke," she said. "I know this has to be hard on you, having to share her all of a sudden."

Brady shrugged. "It's okay. You know, I feel bad for you, remembering how everything happened with me and Josie. I kept thinking to myself that you were ridiculous for being so jealous. But now I get it. I see how strongly they're bonding, and I wonder if she'll still call me Daddy. Then I remember I'm being silly because that's just one more person to love her and take care of her."

He reached out and took her by the hand. "I'm really sorry for any of the things that me and Josie did that made you feel bad when she came back into our lives. Though we've been through a ton of therapy on this, and you said you're good, but I now understand on a deeper level, so I want to apologize to you again."

Maddie shook her head. "You don't owe me any apologies. If anyone should be apologizing, it's me. I was horrible to you back then, and I hurt Kayla in the process. So let's just keep it all firmly in the past, accept that we forgive one another, and ultimately, what we all want is what's best for our daughter. As I told you, you will always be her father. She is just fortunate enough to have another one."

Brady stepped forward and wrapped his arms around her, giving her a big hug. "Thank you," he said. "I hope you realize that I have completely forgiven you for all of the stuff that happened."

He pulled away, looked deep into her eyes. "And I know you, so I know that you are still feeling very guilty over everything with Luke. Don't. We were all just a bunch of dumb kids, doing the best we could, and now you have a wonderful man, doing what he can to make things right. Don't let your bad feelings from the past keep you from moving forward in the future."

Somewhere in the back, someone was calling Brady's name, and he shook his head. "Gotta love impatient teenagers. But take my advice, let go of all the pain from the past. Obviously, we all have a lot of work to do to get our heads right, but our hearts are all in the right place."

He hesitated for a moment, and said, "Though it's none of my business, I see the way you look at each other when you think no one else is looking. Give him a chance. Since you've been working nights, you're not getting as much time with Kayla, but think about maybe taking one of those nights off and going on a date or something with Luke."

Maddie stared at him. "That's a big stretch,"

she said. "I'm sure you mean well, but we don't have that kind of relationship."

She looked back over to the bleachers, where Luke was helping Granny get settled. "Our priority is Kayla, and what's best for her. So don't act like her and Granny and get any ideas about the two of us."

Brady laughed. "If there are three of us trying to get you together, there might be something there. As you mentioned earlier, Kayla is eighteen and an adult. Her life isn't going to end if you and Luke start dating. She could be your biggest cheerleader."

Maddie shrugged. "And if it doesn't work out? Right now, Luke is at our family gatherings, and we can all be a family together. How awkward is that going to be if he and I have a bad breakup and we don't get along anymore?"

Brady shook his head. "The same way we figured it out when we had our share of fights. We all want what's best for Kayla, so even if we don't get along, we will find a way to at least be nice for the sake of our daughter."

"He is not wrong," Luke said, coming up behind her. "The cat's out of the bag, and it's obvious that there's something here. So why don't we try to figure it out to make it work?"

Maddie turned to look at him. "Because of what I just said. I've put Kayla through enough fighting with one of her fathers. I can't do that to her again. I'm sorry."

One of the girls yelled for Brady again, so he turned and grinned at them. "I'm in trouble now," he said. "But seriously, give it some thought. I'd like to think that you're both mature enough that if things don't work out for you romantically, you'll still figure out how to make it work for our daughter."

A tender look crossed Brady's face. "Seriously, Maddie. You deserve a chance at happiness."

Before Maddie could answer, he turned and jogged back toward where the kids were lining up with their horses.

As she turned to make her way back to the stands, Luke stopped her. "Wait."

"I meant what I said," Maddie said.

"I know," he said. "But I also agree with Brady. We are both mature adults who have already agreed that our daughter's needs come first. She keeps dropping hints to me about everything you love and nice things I can do for you. I think she's in favor of the idea, too."

Maddie groaned. "I get it. But you also haven't had eighteen years of your daughter wanting to be like the rest of the kids and having a mommy and daddy who were married, living in the same house as her. It's just a leftover childish fantasy. Don't read more into it than what it is."

This time, when she turned to walk away, he let her. But before she'd taken more than a step, he said, "I don't think this is about the best interests of our daughter. This is more about you and whatever it is that you are afraid of, and having a real relationship. Kayla has already told me that you've never had a serious relationship and only been on a few dates. Maybe, instead of using your excuse, you need to take a long, hard look at what your real motivations are."

Maddie's face burned the entire way to her seat. Who was he to talk to her like that? He didn't even know her. He was just mad because he was interested in her, and she basically turned him down. It was the same thing with every man she tried to date. People told her that she was closed off to romance, but that wasn't true. Her daughter was her most important priority. Her second was her career. She couldn't just push either of those aside for every charming, handsome man who came her way.

Hadn't she grown up with that? Hadn't she experienced the very real pain of being a latchkey kid without a father and a mother who was out every night with a different guy? It was one of the reasons she had been so jealous of Josie. Sure, Josie didn't have a mom, but Josie had had what seemed like the perfect family. Now, of course, Maddie knew that Josie's family was messed up in its own way, and there was no such thing as a perfect family.

Regardless, Maddie understood well enough the damage that having a selfish parent focused on their own happiness could do to a child. She wasn't doing that to her daughter. Maybe in a few years, after Kayla was settled in college, and Maddie was comfortable in her new job, they could think about what a dating relationship would look like.

She glanced over at Luke, who had followed her back to the stands, but was sitting further away from her, closer to his grandmother. But she could tell that whatever Granny had said to him hadn't been encouraging. A dark look covered his face, and Granny looked like the cat who had eaten the canary.

Everyone thought Maddie was resistant to the idea of Luke, but it wasn't true. It was just really bad timing, just like when they first met. It wasn't fair for her to ask him to wait, especially when he pretty much seemed to be champing at the bit. He had only been a father for a few weeks, so he didn't understand the importance of sacrificing for your children.

But as Granny nudged him and said something that brought a smile back to his expression, Maddie wished she had been the one to do that. She wished she could go and sit next to him, but she couldn't afford to cause any more talk about them. Obviously, she needed to work on holding herself more aloof.

What had Luke been thinking, doing something so stupid as to try to get Maddie to see him in a different light? Even days later, Maddie was avoiding him at every turn. He stopped off at the hardware store to pick up a few things he needed for working on Granny's house. Granny's physical therapist didn't feel comfortable releasing her unless the house was made more handicapped-accessible. Not that you could say the *H* word in front of Granny. Even though she was recovering well, she would still need things like safety bars in the shower, and better handrails around the stairs.

And the more he worked on the house, the more he realized just how badly it had fallen into disrepair. At some point, the toilet in the bathroom Granny used the most had developed a leak. It went unnoticed and had rotted the floor. Which was what he was doing here now. Since he had to replace both the floor and the subfloor in the bathroom, he decided to just go ahead and get everything redone. However, they had to special order the parts to create the new bath/shower combo, which had finally come in.

As he watched the employee go to the back to

get the bath/shower combo, Luke realized just how badly he had miscalculated things. There was no way it would fit in his SUV.

Just as he was about to tell the employee that he wouldn't be able to get it today, and he'd have to arrange for alternative transportation, Brady and Wyatt walked up to them.

"Hey, how's it going?" Brady said. "You remember Wyatt, don't you?"

Luke nodded. "Sure do. Good to see you again. I think Kayla is going over to your house to babysit tonight."

Wyatt grinned. "Yes. We got tickets to the Cattlemen's Ball, and I'm excited for me and Laura to get out for a change."

Brady groaned. "I forgot that was tonight. Not only did I not arrange for someone to watch Shana, but Josie is still feeling terrible."

Then he looked over at Luke. "You want to use my tickets? Take Maddie. She loves going, but—"

Wyatt grinned. "That is a great idea. Maddie was a little miffed that we booked Kayla tonight, because she forgot to buy herself a ticket before they sold out, so she was planning on a girls' night watching movies."

It didn't take a rocket scientist to figure out what these two were doing. The hardware store employee came out with his bathtub combo.

"Oh no. I got caught up talking, and I forgot

to come in and tell you that I'm not going to be able to take it home today. It won't fit in my SUV, so I need to find someone with a truck who can help me get home. I hate to make you drag it all the way back in, and I'm really sorry."

Wyatt and Brady slapped him on the back.

"No problem, friend," Brady said. "We're just picking up a couple of parts, so you can save everyone a trip, and we'll just load it up in there."

Wyatt looked over at the clerk. "Cody, you know my truck. I'll pull it up here. We'll get it loaded."

Once again, Luke was struck by the way this family all jumped in to help each other out. He hadn't known how he was going to get someone's truck. But here Brady was, volunteering to take care of it anyway.

"Thank you," Luke said. "Now I don't have to deal with Maddie. Things are weird between us. She's the only one I know with a truck."

Both men laughed and jostled each other. "You're not getting off that easy," Brady said. "As payment for the use of the truck, you have to take us up on that offer for the Cattlemen's Ball."

Luke laughed, shaking his head. "Of course there are strings. Ha ha, you got me. But even if I say yes, it doesn't mean Maddie will."

"Yes, she will," Brady said. "Maddie's favorite event of the year is the Cattlemen's Ball. She wouldn't miss it for the world. And you won't be the one doing the asking, I'm going to call her up and tell her I can't use my ticket."

Luke shook his head. "No offense, but Maddie is already uncomfortable with everyone's attempts at setting us up. So much so that she's been avoiding me. I can't do that to her."

Brady looked over at Wyatt. "You see? I told you he was the salt of the earth. He's the kind of man that we have been praying Maddie would find."

Luke tried not to groan at Brady's pronouncement, but he couldn't help saying, "I appreciate all the prayers, fellas, but nothing is going to happen between me and Maddie. We're both clear on that. Our priority is our daughter."

Even though he didn't like the way Maddie was using her own personal baggage as an excuse to not be with him, the truth was, Luke had enough baggage of his own. How many women had dated him simply because he was a military man, or in the case of his ex-fiancée, because her general daddy told her that he'd make a great husband? He didn't want Maddie to date him because she felt obligated to or because everyone kept pushing them together; he wanted her to date him because she liked him and wanted to be with him.

If anything was going to happen between him and Maddie, it would have to develop on its own time. Though he had moments of attraction to her, and he hated the way she was avoiding him, he wasn't willing to add more drama to their already drama-filled lives.

"All right then, I'll think of a way to get you both to the Cattlemen's Ball," Wyatt said. "I'll grab my truck real quick."

As he walked off, Maddie came toward them. "Hey, guys," she said. "What's this? A family reunion?"

Brady laughed. "Well, you know what they say: the exciting stuff in a small town happens at the hardware store."

Maddie laughed. "Don't forget the ice cream place," she said, smiling. "I'm headed there next to get some sustenance for tonight's project."

Brady grinned. "Yeah, I hear Wyatt stole your date for the night."

Maddie shrugged. "It's okay. I've been wanting to watch that movie for a while, but you know our daughter. She will jump at any chance to make an extra dollar or two. And good for her. I appreciate her go-getter spirit. Just no fun watching romantic comedies by myself."

Luke watched the interplay between Maddie and Brady, and he could tell that Brady was setting her up to go to the Cattlemen's Ball. At least he was here to make sure it was clear he would be taking the other ticket.

"So, you go to the hardware store instead?" Brady asked.

"Yes," Maddie said. "One of the shelves in Kayla's closet is broken, which is one of the reasons her clothes are everywhere, so I'm picking up a few things to fix it and maybe find another organizer or something. Now she won."

Brady's grin told Luke exactly how this was going to play out.

"I have a better idea," Brady said. "Josie isn't feeling well enough to go to the Cattlemen's Ball tonight, so instead of letting our tickets go to waste, what if you go?"

Excitement lit up Maddie's face. "You know I would love to go! It's been ages since I've been to the Cattlemen's Ball! Tickets sell out so fast, and with everything that's been going on, I didn't get the chance to get mine."

"Great," Brady said. "You can ride with Wyatt and Laura. They'll pick you up after they've picked up Luke."

And there it was. The crestfallen look on Maddie's face. Maybe he had been imagining the attraction between the two of them. It made him feel even worse about his words to her the other day. Everyone was pressuring her, and all she wanted was to go about her life.

"You have got to be kidding me," Maddie said. "Your offer wasn't even subtle at all."

Exactly how Luke had seen it. But he hadn't been as wounded by the offer as Maddie clearly was. No wonder she'd been avoiding him.

Brady shrugged. "I know you want to go."

Maddie shook her head. "But you're making it into a date."

Luke could hear the frustration in her voice. He supposed that as wonderful as it could be to have a family to help out, it was tough when they meddled in your business.

Luke smiled at Maddie. "Look, it doesn't have to be a date. We'd be going as a group of friends and to be honest, I'm not even sure I should go. I don't have anything to wear to a ball, except my mess dress."

At least it got a laugh out of Maddie. "It's not like a ball on TV," she said. "It's the annual fund-raiser for our Cattlemen's Association, and while it does give us all a chance to dress up, for the men, it can range from a suit to a nice pair of jeans, a dress shirt, and a Western hat. If I remember correctly, mess dress is your fancy military uniform, and I've seen plenty of people in those."

That was one of the many things he liked about Maddie. Even though she obviously didn't want to go with him, she was still trying to help him feel comfortable if he chose to go.

"Does that mean it's okay if we go together?"

He saw the hesitation on her face, so he quickly added, "As friends, of course."

Maddie rewarded him with a smile. "I guess. Miles Jeffries always does the best smoked brisket, and all of his sides are on point. You have to go for the food alone. You definitely haven't lived until you've tried the amazing food at this event."

Wyatt pulled up in his truck. He called out the window, "Let's get you loaded up." Then he noticed Maddie. "Did you talk to her about tonight?"

Brady puffed out his chest like he'd won a major event. "She's in," he said.

The other men might think it was a victory, but he could tell from the expression on Maddie's face that this was likely going to make things even more difficult between the two of them.

"Were you in on this?" she asked, looking at Luke.

"I was ambushed just like you," he told her honestly. "And I told them you weren't going to appreciate the interference. I meant what I said. If this is going to make things difficult for you, then I won't go. Unlike you, I don't know what I'm missing."

Maddie's shoulders rose and fell like she was letting out a long sigh. "I must seem like I'm being overly sensitive, but I've worked hard to get where I am and to repair my reputation. I thought I was finally there, but all this stuff with Briana..."

Her voice trailed off, and she didn't need to finish the sentence. Despite his gains with Briana over Granny's diet and sharing recipes, she still seemed eager to find fault with everything, and made snide comments about Maddie every chance she got.

"I get it," he said. "Just remember that everyone else is being supportive, and as I've heard your boss say multiple times, you've done nothing wrong. I promise I'll do everything I can tonight to keep tongues from wagging. Let's just go have a good time."

Maddie nodded slowly, then smiled. "It really is good brisket."

She gestured at the men getting ready to load the tub fixture in the truck. "You should probably go help them. I'll see you tonight."

Even though she said going to the Cattlemen's Ball with him was no big deal, she said she'd see him tonight with all the enthusiasm of someone headed to get a root canal.

Hopefully, they'd find a way to have a good time. At the very least, as Maddie said, he'd be in for a good meal.

But there was a part of him that was disappointed it wasn't something more.

Chapter Seven

Why did Maddie feel so giddy at the idea of going to the Cattlemen's Association Ball? She'd been to the event many times before, and it was always the same thing: mingle with their friends and have hors d'oeuvres when they arrived, then go to their tables, where they'd be served a nice dinner—no, a feast—catered by the J Bar W Ranch and their prime beef. Everyone looked forward to that meal. It was probably the best meal she'd have all year, so her nerves weren't about that. Instead, she was standing in front of the mirror, fussing over her appearance for another reason.

"Please tell me you're not wearing that ugly old thing," Kayla said.

Maddie turned and looked at her daughter. "What's wrong with this? It's my best dress."

Kayla groaned. "Exactly. You've worn that dress for as long as I can remember."

Maddie shrugged. "Well, it's all I have. I'm not like you, with my closets overflowing."

Kayla gave the usual teenage eye roll. Maddie was used to it. "Not really, considering you made me give away a bunch of stuff."

Then Kayla's face brightened. "Hey, wait a second. In those dresses I tossed into the giveaway box, there's one I ordered off the internet. It was too big, and they wouldn't take it back. It'll fit you."

Before Maddie could answer, Kayla dashed off, then returned with a flowing pink princess dress. Maddie remembered that one all right. She'd told Kayla no because it was too fancy, and that if she wanted the dress, Kayla would have to buy it herself. Maddie had also said no because it was from an online retailer. She had warned Kayla that many of those places were often scams.

Kayla had insisted, and Maddie told her that it was fine, as long as Kayla spent her own money and was prepared to be disappointed. Her daughter had cried that day when the dress arrived, a couple sizes too big, and Maddie had consoled her, saying that they could probably get it taken in somewhere, but then one of Kayla's friends had offered her a different dress, so it had languished in the back of Kayla's closet instead.

"It's perfect for you," Kayla said.

Maddie looked at her suspiciously. "No offense, but that's not really my style, and it's way too fancy."

Kayla snorted. "I'm on the same social media as you. I know what other people wear to the Cattlemen's Ball. This dress will fit in nicely. And it's far better than your usual ugly black thing."

In truth, Maddie hadn't loved the idea of wearing the same tired black dress she wore to every function. But it wasn't like she had the time or extra money to get something else. All her money went to caring for her daughter, which meant there wasn't anything left to buy fancy dresses she'd wear maybe once a year.

With nothing to lose, Maddie took the dress to the bathroom to try on. She didn't think of herself as much of a pink person, but this shade of pink looked good against Maddie's skin, and even though Maddie had thought it was not really her style, she had to admit she couldn't remember the last time she'd worn such a flowing gown.

"Mom!"

Maddie grudgingly came out of the bathroom, knowing she was going to hear Kayla say, "I told you so."

But instead, her daughter's eyes widened. "Wow," she said. "Mom, you're…"

The surprise in her daughter's voice made Maddie laugh. At one time, Maddie might have wanted to think she was hot, but now she was just a woman approaching middle age, hoping that maybe she might look nice.

"We have got to do the whole thing," Kayla said. "We don't need to leave for Wyatt's for another thirty minutes. I can get you even more glammed up."

Maddie gave her daughter a look. She wasn't sure she wanted Kayla's idea of glammed up, but before she could protest, Kayla said, "Have you ever seen me wear makeup that you didn't like on me? Just because you don't do yourself up often doesn't mean you shouldn't once in a while."

As much as Maddie hated to admit it, Kayla was right. She couldn't recall a time when her daughter had walked out of the house with hair and makeup that she thought was inappropriate. Everyone always complimented Kayla on her appearance, so it wasn't really what Maddie was nervous about.

"People will think I'm trying too hard," Maddie said.

"So what? You're the one who always tells me not to care about what other people think. As long as you're acting with integrity, who cares?"

Fine time for her daughter to use her words against her. But there was a huge difference between what people thought of Kayla, and how they'd always treated Maddie. What if Briana was there, and saw Maddie dressed to the nines? And then there was Luke…

"Wait till Dad gets a load of this."

"Exactly." Maddie pulled away from Kayla's ministrations.

"Stay still," Kayla said firmly.

Maddie took a deep breath. They had to address this. "Honey, I know you and Granny are trying to get me and your dad together, but neither of us are ready for a relationship right now. So if you're doing this in hopes that your father will look at me and fall in love, just stop. We're just using Brady and Josie's extra tickets. Going as friends, with friends. Just like you do for your school dances."

Kayla groaned. "That's only because I can never get a date. And because if I did get a date, Dad would totally freak out."

Maddie grinned. Brady definitely had strong opinions on what kind of boy his daughter was allowed to be around, even if she was eighteen. But he only wanted what was best for his daughter, so Maddie had always told Kayla to give him a little grace.

"Mom, you never go out on dates. If you worry that it's going to upset me, don't. I'm worried about what you're going to do when I go to college. I would feel a lot better about going away to school if you had someone to keep you company."

Her daughter's heart was in the right place, and even though it wasn't Kayla's job to worry about whether or not Maddie was lonely when she went off to college, it was so sweet.

But dating now, and especially Luke…this was the wrong time to be thinking about such things.

"I promise," Maddie said. "As soon as you go off to school, I'll join one of those dating apps."

Kayla tugged at her hair a little too hard with the brush. "Ow!"

"Sorry," Kayla said. "Why would you need to sign up for one of those apps when you have a perfectly good man staring you in the face? Not that I'm supposed to notice anything, but my dad is pretty cute for being a dad."

Her daughter was impossible.

"That may be so, but I don't want to pick a date based on how good they look. I need a chance to get to know a person and find out about their character first. Luke is a good enough guy, but just because he's good as a father doesn't necessarily make him a good romantic partner. After all, that's why Brady and I never worked out."

Kayla stepped back from her. "Yeah, but you and Brady Dad never had any kind of sparks. I've never seen him look at you the way Luke Dad looks at you."

Busted. But this wasn't an appropriate conversation to have with her daughter. Especially since Kayla had too many romantic notions in her head to understand the level of sacrifice a real relationship took.

"I think you're trying to see things that aren't there because you want so badly for us all to be a family. I'm not ready to be in a relationship right now, and I need you to accept that."

As always with her daughter when they disagreed, the fight shone in Kayla's eyes.

"Why should I?" Kayla said. "Look, you always sacrificed for me. I remember times when I was younger, and someone would ask you out to dinner or a movie or something, and you'd always say something like, 'Oh, sorry, I have Kayla.'"

For a moment, Kayla looked genuinely upset. Then she said, "But maybe the real reason you told all those people that is because there was a part of you that always loved my father. Please give him a chance."

How was Maddie supposed to tell her daughter that this romantic notion she'd built up over Maddie and Luke loving each other all these years was just a fantasy?

Kayla held up a mirror to Maddie's face. "There you go. All finished."

Maddie almost didn't recognize herself in the mirror. Even though she'd known that Kayla wasn't going to turn her into a painted lady, she hadn't expected the subtle but artful way the makeup had been applied to her face.

Her eyes were highlighted in the stylish way for teenagers, but didn't make her look like an adult who was trying too hard. The rest of her makeup was subtle, classy, and made Maddie think she was staring at a younger woman in the mirror. Kayla had also found some shoes that matched Maddie's dress. If Maddie had chosen a look for herself, this is what she'd have chosen. Maybe her daughter knew her after all.

"I look amazing. Thank you." Maddie smiled at her daughter, then held her arms out. "You think I can have a hug?"

Kayla grumbled. "I suppose, since I know you'll just pout, like you do when I hug Granny and my dad."

"Why should they get hugs and not me?"

"You've been hugging me my whole life, and they need to catch up."

But then Kayla came and gave her a hug. A real hug, and even though Maddie had been mourning the loss of her little girl, seeing the woman she was becoming brought a new feeling of joy to her heart.

The alarm on Kayla's phone beeped. "That's my reminder," Kayla said. "We need to get over to Wyatt's so I can babysit, and you can ride with them to the ball."

They had all agreed that it would be easier for everyone to meet at Wyatt's and ride together.

Parking at the Cattlemen's Ball was always at a premium, so carpooling made sense.

"I can't wait to see the look on Dad's face when he sees you."

As much as Maddie wanted to remind her daughter once again that this was not happening, they just had such a beautiful moment that she couldn't spoil it.

When they got to Wyatt and Laura's, Maddie began to feel self-conscious. Sure, Kayla had said she looked good, but that was the opinion of a teenage girl. Had she overdone it? She didn't want to be one of those older women trying to look young.

But when she walked through the door, Laura's face lit up. "Wow, you look incredible."

"Yeah," Wyatt said. "You look nice. If we hadn't already lined up a date for you, I'd say you're going to have all kinds of heads turning."

"We only want Dad to notice her," Kayla said emphatically.

"Stop, both of you," Maddie said. "This is not a real date. Don't put ideas into people's heads that don't belong there. Luke and I are just co-parents, and maybe friends."

Kayla gave another annoyed groan. "I'm going to check on the little ones," she said. "They're being awfully quiet, and the last time that happened when I was over here, they had just painted the bathroom mirror with Laura's new lipstick."

As everyone laughed, Kayla started for the back of the house where the kids were, but then she paused. "You just keep working on her about my dad. Mom is getting on my nerves with how stubborn she is."

"Kayla," Maddie said. "You're really crossing the line into being disrespectful today."

Kayla grinned. "I'm only speaking the truth in love."

Before Maddie could chastise her daughter again, Kayla had skipped off into the bedrooms.

"I need to check something in the kitchen for a minute," Laura said. "Come with me."

As Maddie followed Laura into the kitchen, she said, "I know Wyatt isn't going to be any help, but I really needed to be supported here. I don't want a romantic relationship with Luke."

The doorbell rang, and Wyatt went to answer it. Laura looked at Maddie. "Why not? Wyatt keeps commenting that there's obviously something between you two. Everyone else sees it. Maybe you should stop fighting it and just see where it goes?"

"Come on, Laura. You know why. I can't risk hurting my daughter again. She's happy and excited now, but what if we do get together? Then we break up, and it's going to hurt her."

"Can we stop with that?" Luke said, entering the room. "You're using fear to not allow yourself a chance at happiness based on a lot of what-ifs, and you have no evidence of what will actually happen. I thought you were a woman of faith. But that isn't how a woman of faith talks. I was willing to give this a try. The more I hear you argue against it, the more I'm not sure I would want to date someone who lives her life in so much fear."

Then he looked her up and down. "I'm supposed to tell you how beautiful you look tonight because I understand Kayla went to a lot of trouble. And I'll tell her that. I'll tell you that. But I hope you know, you've always been beautiful to me, no matter what you wear."

He turned his attention to Wyatt. "So, when does the shindig start anyway? I'm starving."

Even though she had been telling herself all night that Luke's opinion didn't matter to her, his easy dismissal of her stung. This is what she wanted. For her Luke to be just friends.

The cold way he'd just spoken to her about her faith made her heart hurt, and it felt like there was a greater distance between them than there had ever been. But if this was the price she had to pay, then she'd pay it. Everyone might think she was acting out of fear, but she was no longer that reckless girl who thrived on taking risks. Her daughter was everything to her, and Maddie was never going to do something that would harm her daughter.

She'd already done that once, by revealing the truth about Kayla's paternity in a moment of anger. Though they had worked through it as a family, and Maddie knew Kayla had forgiven her, Maddie would never forget the lesson she'd learned.

Even though Luke had questioned Maddie's faith, Maddie closed her eyes and prayed that God would give her the strength to handle the situation. She'd cried out to God so many times over the years, and it seemed like now, with everyone pushing her in a direction that could cause more pain, she needed His strength even more.

Maybe he shouldn't have said that about her faith. Luke was painfully aware of how stiffly she stood next to him at the Cattlemen's Ball. He just didn't understand why this woman who seemed to have everything going for her would be so afraid to take a chance on love.

But maybe it was better this way. He'd thought things would be easier once he got out of the army and women weren't afraid of his dangerous job. Yet here he was, attracted to a woman who'd made it quite clear she wasn't interested in him. Even though he'd called her out on her excuses, it didn't matter what the excuses were. The bottom line was that she didn't want to date him, and he needed to leave it alone.

He stole another glance at Maddie. He had not been lying when he told her that he thought she was beautiful. She looked like the belle of the ball. He kinda liked her better in her scrubs. She always found something fun to wear and used her outfits as another way of keeping people's spirits up. He liked that about her. But he couldn't express that to her. He wanted to say a lot of the things to her, but because he'd already messed things up, he felt like he couldn't. Still, he should've been more complimentary about the dress.

"You look really nice tonight," he said. "I should've made a bigger deal about it than I did because I know it's special."

She gave him a funny look, like she wasn't sure why he was bothering now.

"And I'm sorry about what I said about your fear and your faith. That was out of line. Your reasons are your reasons, and I need to respect them, just like everyone else should."

Maddie gave a small smile. "Thank you."

Finally. Progress. At least her posture had softened, and she didn't look like she wanted to run as far away as possible from an event she'd been looking forward to.

"It's not you, you know," she said slowly. "I'm sure you'd be a great person to date. It's just not where I'm at in my life right now."

The firmness in her voice made him realize

just how hard it was on her to have everyone pushing her to date. All she really wanted was for people to respect her and her wishes. He'd messed that up tonight.

"I get it," he said. "In all honesty, I should probably figure out my own life priorities first as well. In just a few short weeks, it seems like my whole life has changed."

She gave him a tender smile. "And you're doing great managing it."

For a moment, it looked like she wanted to say something else, but a woman came up to them and greeted Maddie warmly.

"I'm so glad to see you here," she said. "I feel like it's been ages since I've seen you at the senior center. It's always fun catching up with you when you pop in to check on Mom."

Though Maddie smiled, it didn't light up her eyes the way her smiles usually did. Probably because the reason she hadn't seen her friend was due to all the trouble Briana had caused. "It's great to see you, too, Sadie."

Then Maddie gestured at Luke. "Have you met Luke? He's Ida Mae's grandson, freshly out of the army. Luke, this is my friend Sadie."

Sadie smiled and held out her hand. "It's a pleasure to meet you. Ida Mae is one of Mom's crafting buddies. I can't tell you how happy it has made your grandmother to have you home."

Then she looked slyly over at Maddie before turning her attention back to him. "And to think you've been Kayla's father all along. What a great blessing for everyone. From what your grandmother tells my mom, I hear we may be dancing at a wedding soon. The Cattlemen's Ball is a great place to practice."

This was definitely not what Luke wanted to hear, especially after he and Maddie had seemingly made their peace over the matchmaking issue.

"Well, I'm sure we'll all be happy to see who the bride and groom are," Luke said, smiling. "But if Granny is trying to match me up with someone, she's in for a rude awakening. I'm afraid getting married, or even dating, isn't part of my plan right now. I have two priorities: my daughter and getting the house fixed up so Granny can come home."

Though he'd been telling himself those were his priorities all along, saying that to a would-be matchmaker made Luke feel even better about his conversation with Maddie. This wasn't the best time for him to be thinking about dating.

Sadie looked puzzled, then glanced over at Maddie. "I thought you two had gotten back together."

Maddie shook her head. "I'm afraid that's just wishful thinking on Ida Mae's part. Like Luke, my priority is my daughter, and the next priority is my job. Between the two, I'm afraid I don't have much time for romance."

Sadie laughed. "Oh, trust me. I get it. My mom gives my name and number to every handsome man who comes into the senior center to visit a relative. I know our families just want us to be happy, but they need to let us make our own paths."

"Hear, hear," Luke said as enthusiastically as he could. He wanted Maddie to know he was on her side.

"I know you're not on the market, but the band is getting ready to play a few songs. Do you think we could dance?" Sadie asked.

Even though Maddie had told him vehemently how much she didn't want to date him, he couldn't help noticing the way she flinched at the question.

"I'm afraid I've got two left feet," Luke said. "That's the other reason why there won't be anyone dancing at my wedding anytime soon."

As Sadie turned away, Maddie said quietly, "You don't need to turn anyone down on my account. We're just here as friends, so you can dance with whoever you like."

Luke shrugged. "There's only one woman here I want to dance with," he said. "And not only has she made her feelings about me painfully clear, but given the talk that's already happening, and how uncomfortable it makes her, I wouldn't want to give any more reason for people's tongues to wag."

Her expression softened slightly. "Like I said, it's not personal." She gestured at the crowded room. "It's just life in this town. All these people have looked down on me for one reason or another. First it was because my mom was such a mess and I didn't have a dad. Then I got pregnant as a teenager, and became the typical statistic."

His stomach churned at the pregnancy reference. She always seemed to blame herself, yet he was equally to blame.

But he didn't want to interrupt her as she continued, "I was the horrible woman who ruined Brady's life, and created drama when Josie came home. And then, just when I was finally feeling like I was getting past all the bad things people said about me, you arrive, and it's back to square one."

Wow. He hadn't considered how everything they were going through now had brought up so much of Maddie's past.

The band began playing a lively song, and even though it didn't match Luke's and Maddie's moods, everyone else moved toward the stage, giving them a little more privacy in the crowded room. Still, he took her by the arm and led her to a more secluded corner to get away from the noise, and allow Maddie to get this off her chest.

Maddie's eyes filled with tears as she said, "I finally have my chance at redemption and proving them all wrong. My daughter is ready to graduate high school and go to college and be successful despite everything everyone ever said about how I'd never raise a good child as a single mom. I'm hopeful about getting the promotion at my job that I've always dreamed of. I'm making a real difference in people's lives. I can't afford to have anything mess that up."

That was probably the most real thing she had said to him about why she couldn't date him. Sure, she'd given her reasons about Kayla, and he believed that was one of her concerns. But as he saw the pain on her face, he understood that it was about so much more.

Luke could relate. Hadn't he spent his whole life trying to prove himself worthy to his family? The weight of all the medals adorning his mess dress pressed against his chest. He'd thought that all the decorations and medals would be enough. Even his second purple heart hadn't gotten his father to say, "I'm proud of you."

His dad was long gone, but as soon as Luke came home, he was still the black sheep who had ruined everyone's lives.

No, not everyone's. Just Briana's. No matter

what he did, it seemed she would always hate him. Sure, they'd come to some level of detente, and he was doing his best work on their relationship. But he still felt the weight of her disapproving glare whenever they were in Granny's room.

"I get it," he said. "Maybe you should tell that to Granny and Kayla."

Maddie shook her head. "I can't. Sometimes kids at school pick on Kayla, so I'm constantly telling her not to worry about what others think."

"Then why don't you take your own advice?"

Luke stopped a passing waiter to grab a bottle of water for each of them. They could both use the distraction of a drink, and he was parched.

Maddie accepted the water with a smile, took a long drink, then sighed. "Because unlike Kayla, I have done a lot of things wrong. I don't deserve all the things people have said about me over the years, but let's be honest. Some of them I did deserve. I've been trying to be a better person, but I can never seem to escape my past."

If only they weren't in a room full of the people Maddie was so afraid of judging her. Luke wanted to hug her and let her know he understood.

He hadn't been a good person back when he'd first met Maddie, either. It seemed like they had both worked so hard to move past those old identities. The Bible said they were all new creations in Christ.

So why, if both he and Maddie had changed, couldn't others see that in them?

Instead, he said softly, "I know how that feels. After all, you've seen how Briana still treats me over all the mistakes I've made."

Maddie nodded sympathetically. "So you see why I have to do everything right. I've worked too hard to ruin it now."

He could tell she was on the verge of tears, so he gestured at the door. "Why don't we go outside and get some fresh air?"

Maddie nodded, and they walked out into a courtyard decorated with twinkling lights. Part of him wished things were different so he could comment on how romantic it was and share a special moment with her. But he couldn't be that for her; he could only be a friend.

They found a secluded area decorated with hay bales arranged as seating for guests. A breeze picked up, and Maddie shivered, so Luke shrugged out of his jacket. "Here. Put this on."

Maddie looked up at him as if to remind him that it would only give people something to talk about.

"I'd rather people talk than you freeze. Put it on," Luke said firmly.

A soft smile lit up Maddie's face. "Am I that obvious?"

Luke shrugged. "Maybe. But like you said, I get it. I keep thinking about Briana and how angry she is with me over the past. How much longer do I have to pay for something I did as a kid? What is the timeline for how long someone should pay for their sins?"

Maddie shrugged. "I don't know. It feels like forever."

Luke looked down at the ground, thinking about the verse that had come to him earlier about being a new creation in Christ. "It does, but then I wonder about God and Jesus, and how our sins were forgiven on the cross. How long does the Bible say we're supposed to pay for what we've done?"

Maddie rewarded him with a gentle laugh. "You know, I've never quite thought about that. What we're taught in churches is that we're forgiven once and for all."

"Yeah," he said, looking down at the ground, wondering why he didn't just accept that forgiveness. Why neither of them could. Here he was, trying to give good advice to Maddie, but he needed to take it as well.

"I guess it's easier said than done," he finally said. "It makes it a lot harder when people are constantly rubbing your nose in your past."

The understanding expression on Maddie's face gave him hope. "Exactly. I just want prove to all the people who said I was a good-for-nothing and I'd come to a bad end that they were wrong about me."

"And who are those people?" Luke asked.

Maddie shrugged. "I'd like to say no one that matters, but I guess I let them matter."

"For what it's worth," he said, "it seems to me that the people in your life who matter, like Brady and his family, and Kayla, they don't seem to hold it against you."

Maddie appeared to be processing his words, nodding slowly, and then he said, "You should also know that I've never held your mistakes against you, either. You did what you had to do, and I'm really grateful that thanks to everything you've done, we have a really amazing daughter."

Maddie rewarded him with another smile. "I've always been grateful that in spite of my mistakes, God has chosen to bless me so richly."

Even though Luke had been using this conversation to make Maddie feel better, he was actually starting to see how much it was helping him. All this time, he'd been angry with himself and blamed himself for his mistakes. Yet despite everything he'd done wrong, the most important person in his life, his Granny, thought the world of him. And somehow, he'd also ended up with a wonderful daughter who loved him. Those were the people who mattered most in his life, and they didn't hold anything against him.

In fact, God loved him on an even deeper level. For the first time since coming home, Luke felt the weight of all his sins fall off him. He had nothing to prove to anyone, especially not God, and it was God's opinion that mattered the most.

Before he could share this revelation with Maddie, Briana walked up.

"Well, well, well. If it isn't two little lovebirds who say they aren't lovebirds."

Luke glanced between himself and Maddie. They might be sitting next to each other, but there was plenty of space between them, and save the fact that Maddie was wearing his jacket, no one would have thought anything of it.

"Why don't you mind your own business?" he said. "We came out for a bit of air, and Maddie was chilly, so I did what any gentleman would do, and I offered her my jacket."

Briana looked Maddie up and down. "Shouldn't you be at work? I thought they moved you to nights."

Maddie glared at Briana. "If you were so familiar with my schedule, you'd know that tonight is my normal night off."

Unfortunately, her words didn't sway Briana at all. "And I thought it had been made perfectly clear that you aren't supposed to be fraternizing with patients' families."

Pulling Luke's jacket around her, Maddie stood. "That is not true. There is nothing in the employee handbook that says I can't talk to Luke outside of work. Both me and Claire made sure of that."

This was beyond ridiculous. They shouldn't have to deal with Briana's harassment like this, especially since this had nothing to do with Granny.

"Look," Luke said. "I know I hurt you in the past. I'm sorry for everything I've done. You were my best friend when we were kids. I can't change what happened, but we can change how we treat each other in the future."

He expected Briana to make a smart comment, but she remained silent, so he continued. "We both want what's best for Granny. So does Maddie. I don't know why you don't like Maddie. She's been nothing but good to Granny, and that's what should matter."

"You don't know her like I do," Briana said.

He could feel Maddie stiffen beside him.

"What did she ever do to you?" Luke asked.

Briana shrugged. "She has a terrible reputation."

That wasn't an answer, and they all knew it. But it only confirmed the fears Maddie had confessed to him earlier.

"Until I came home, did you have any complaints about how Maddie cared for Granny?"

Briana didn't answer.

"And has anyone at the senior center ever complained about how Maddie helps others?"

Again, no answer.

Luke squared his shoulders and looked at Maddie, then back at Briana. "I realize I haven't been here very long, and I don't know all the history. But what I do know is that every person I talk to in this town tells me what a great job Maddie does at the senior center and how she's helped someone they know, including Granny. So stop with the personal attacks and the attacks on her competency. This isn't what your treatment of Maddie is about, and it's time you stopped bullying her."

Briana looked like Luke had just thrown a bucket of ice water on her, and he was glad. He didn't know why it had taken so long to stand up to her, but this was the first time they'd encountered Briana outside the senior center. Maddie probably would have stopped him had he done so there.

Briana's husband, Corey, walked up to them. "There you are. Luke, good to see you again. Nice night, isn't it?"

He placed a kiss on his wife's cheek, then seemed to notice the tension.

"Fighting about Granny again?" he asked.

Briana sent Luke a glare, then said, "I have a headache. I want to go home."

"Of course." Corey held his arm out to Briana.

Once Briana and Corey were out of earshot, Maddie said, "Thank you. You shouldn't have said that, because I'm sure it will cause trouble later, but it was nice to have someone stand up for me. Not many people have been willing to do that."

Maddie didn't often show this vulnerable side, and he could see how it had taken a lot of courage and trust for her to share as deeply with him as she had tonight.

"No," he said. "I should have said it to her sooner. I meant what I said. You said earlier that Kayla hadn't done anything to deserve it when people were mean to her. You've done nothing to deserve how Briana treats you."

All this time, Maddie had been working to encourage their daughter, because Kayla was a good kid who didn't deserve to be picked on. Maddie thought she deserved it because of her past mistakes, but as far as Luke could tell, she'd already made up for them.

"It doesn't matter," Maddie said. "In Briana's eyes, I'll always be the worthless girl who got pregnant out of wedlock and ruins people's lives because of it. I may not have done anything to her, but now she sees me and my daughter as a threat to her relationship with Granny."

Unfortunately, that part was true. But as the lights shone in Maddie's tear-filled eyes, there was one thing Luke could disagree with.

"You aren't a worthless girl. Never have been. Never will be. Surely you know that."

Maddie looked at the ground. "I want to believe it. But at what point will people stop treating me like I am?"

"When you stop letting them." He took her by the hand. "When you stop thinking that you somehow deserve it."

He thought about the wisdom from the Bible and the forgiveness of sins that he'd wanted to share with her earlier.

"Do you believe God forgives you?" he asked.

"Of course." A peaceful look crossed Maddie's face. "My faith is all I've had to cling to at times."

The breeze kicked up, and even Luke was getting a bit chilly. But before he suggested going back inside, he said, "Then who cares what they think? If you're living for God's approval, that's all that matters."

She looked like she was going to argue, but he shook his head. "Yes, I know, Briana is trying to get you fired. And I promise, I'll do everything I can to prevent that. I promise, I will stand up for you."

The tears that had been shining in her eyes started to roll down her cheeks.

Luke reached forward and brushed them aside. "But you have to promise me something."

"What?"

"No more avoiding me. We're not doing anything wrong. And for the sake of our daughter, we need to communicate and spend time together."

Maddie looked doubtful. "But the matchmaking…"

"I'll help you make it clear that people need to stop. I humored everyone, but I can see now that you needed me to back you up more strongly."

More tears fell, and Luke pulled a handkerchief out of his pocket and handed it to her.

"Let's move forward, Maddie. Together."

She dabbed at her eyes and nodded. "Okay."

Once again, he'd have liked to hug her. Instead, he squeezed her hand and said, "I'm here for you. I can't change the past, but I'm here for you now."

The warmth he felt from Maddie told him that he'd finally gotten through to her. It didn't solve the problem of Briana, but at least now, Maddie wouldn't be avoiding him, and whatever came their way, they'd figure out together.

Chapter Eight

This was more like it. Maddie sat back on the porch swing at the main ranch house at Shepherd's Creek, sipping her lemonade. Sometimes Maddie marveled at how easily they could all be family, considering everything in the past. Funny how all those years, Maddie had envied Josie for her family, and now Maddie was a part of it. In that spirit, they were including Luke and his family as well.

Maddie grinned as she saw the little ones crawling all over Granny. She knew that Granny's dearest wish had always been to have more grandchildren and great-grandchildren to spoil. While she definitely wasn't going to be giving in to Granny's pressure to have more children, it was nice to see that Granny could fulfill her need for children in a different way. In fact, Granny was probably getting an overload with Wyatt and Laura's three toddler boys, and Josie's toddler daughter.

Luke sat beside her. "Every time I think it's

not possible for Granny to be any happier, something happens to surprise me. Maybe this will get her off our backs about giving her more great-grandchildren."

Maddie laughed. "Funny, I was thinking the same thing."

He gestured at Laura handing Granny a glass of lemonade. "Should she be having that? I know we're supposed to be watching her sugar intake."

Maddie shrugged. "It's fine. The family has always been conscious of healthy eating and minimizing the amount of sugar in things."

She watched as Granny took a deep, appreciative sip of the drink. "Besides, you can't control everything she does."

Luke nodded. "I know. I just want her home so bad. And I'm afraid of anything that would mess that up for her. I'm not faulting the care that she gets at the senior center. If I had to be in a place like that, I'd want to be in one you run. But I can't stand seeing her so unhappy, and if this is what it will take to get her home, I'm willing to do it."

Maddie appreciated Luke's dedication. But before she could comment on it, Brady came toward them from the barn, and the kids ran to him.

"Ride?" they all shouted in unison.

Brady's loud laugh made her giggle. "All right," he said. "We've got Stolley Bear saddled for you, and we'll all take turns."

Maddie looked at Luke. "Even though they have all these horses, it's actually a rare treat to let the little ones ride. It's too much work to keep them all corralled and out of mischief."

Maddie brought her attention to Granny. "You want to go with us? I know how much you love Stolley Bear, especially now that we found out he's related to Caramello."

Granny grinned. "Do you think I could ride, too?"

Maddie hesitated. Though Granny was making great strides in her physical therapy, she hadn't heard that Granny was cleared to ride.

"I'm not sure about that, Granny," Luke said. "I know that technically your hip is healed, but you're still supposed to take it easy."

Then he gestured at her cane. "We got you out of your walker, but you're still not fully getting around on your own. I'm not sure how safe it would be for you."

Brady joined them. "We could do like we do with the little ones. She can sit on the saddle, and one of us will lead her around the arena."

Granny looked at them both wistfully. "Please? You know how much I've been wanting to ride."

Maddie wanted to tell the old woman yes. They had a stool that would help her mount, and all she would need to do was sit in the saddle. But if something happened and Briana found out, Maddie's job would be on the line for sure.

"I think I need to bow out of this decision," Maddie said, taking a step back. "I can't say yes, and I can't say no."

She could feel the weight of Granny's disappointment, and even Luke was looking at her funny, but then he nodded like he understood.

"Granny, you know that if anything happens and Briana finds out, she's going to get Maddie in trouble. Maybe even me. Can't you see that we all are trying to get you home? Once that happens, I promise I will take you here anytime you want as long as they're willing to help you ride. But not for now."

Granny's eyes filled with tears. "What if I don't get to go home?"

"Of course you will," Maddie said. "The staff is doing a great job helping you, and you're working so hard to do all the things you're supposed to. And Luke, too. Everyone's doing their part, so you just have to have a little more faith."

"Please," Granny said.

Brady looked at Granny with tenderness and love in his eyes. "Ida Mae, I have known you my whole life. While I believe that you are completely safe, I also know that these two are just trying to do their best for you. I give you my word that once you are released to go, I will drop everything and I will take you for a ride."

Maddie smiled at Granny. "We can plan a family trail ride."

The disappointment on Granny's face was real, but she nodded slowly.

"I don't want to make any trouble. I know how hard everyone is working to get me home. I don't know why Briana is being so mean, but if she gets you fired, I will cut her out of my will."

Maddie shook her head. "Don't you dare. Her insecurity is what's causing her to act like this, so let's instead think about ways we can make Briana feel more secure. It would go a long way if you told her that you had the opportunity to ride, and we told you no."

"Fine," Granny said. "I guess it won't hurt me to wait a little while longer. Let's go watch those kids. I do love the sound of a child's laughter on a horse."

Garrett, one of the twins, ran up to Luke and extended his arms. "Ride."

Luke grinned. "Yes, we're going to the barn now."

The little boy shook his head gestured up at Luke. "Ride."

Maddie held her arms out to the little boy. "I can give you a piggyback ride," she said.

"Well, if that's what you wanted," Luke said,

"I'm happy to oblige." He bent down and let the little boy climb onto his back.

Even though Maddie was used to this kind of behavior, and she'd seen the different men at Shepherd's Creek giving dozens of piggyback rides, she'd never seen Luke have the opportunity to interact with the little ones. As they all went to the barn, Maddie couldn't help noticing the way the boy on Luke's shoulders chattered to him, and Luke seemed to be responding.

She had no idea what they were talking about, but it made her heart melt. A pang of regret hit her as she realized that Luke had never gotten to experience this with Kayla, but maybe someday when Kayla married and had children of her own, he could at least be a grandfather to her kids.

Even though Granny still walked with a cane, there was an extra spring in her step as she kept up with everyone headed to the barn. Being here at the stables probably did more for Granny's rehabilitation than the hours in the gym.

That was the thing about Maddie's dreams of being director at the senior center. It wasn't just the idea of upward mobility in her career, but the fact that she truly loved her job, and she was invested in the lives of the people who came through their doors. Granny was special to her, not just because she was Kayla's great-grandmother, but because Maddie enjoyed her as a person.

When they got to the barn, they all went out behind it to the round pen. Brady and Wyatt had set everything up for the kids to ride. When it came time for the twin that Luke had on his shoulders, as he lifted the eager little boy off, the boy kicked him in the face, causing Luke's nose to bleed.

Someone handed him a napkin, and Maddie grabbed him by the arm. "Let's get you into the first aid room and we'll get you taken care of."

Maddie led him into the first aid room in the barn, which was kept fully stocked in case of minor injuries. "Why don't you come in here and sit down for a moment so we can get the bleeding to stop."

Luke groaned. "I'm not hurt that badly," he said. "It's just a bloody nose."

Maddie shook her head. "He kicked you pretty hard. And I can see that it's already starting to swell. Humor me and sit here with an ice pack on it for a little bit. Here's a cloth to catch the blood. If you give me a hard time, I'll make you go to urgent care."

For a moment, he got the same argumentative look on his face that Granny did when Maddie tried to advise her to do something for her own good, but as Luke stood, the fight went out of him. Yes, he was injured worse than he was giving himself credit for. This wasn't Maddie's first rodeo, and if she wasn't mistaken, Luke would have quite the shiner tomorrow.

Maddie opened the freezer and grabbed an ice pack, then handed it to him.

With kids, horses, and all sorts of other animals and dangers, they had everything they needed for a nosebleed.

"Who knew your nursing skills could be used on someone other than the elderly," Luke said, giving a small laugh.

"Oh, you'd be surprised. We have a team of volunteer first-aid personnel at the stables watching every ride, just in case. We take safety very seriously here and are prepared for just about everything." Then she gestured toward the outer walls. "And, for the rare occasion, the ambulance isn't that far away."

Luke removed the cloth from his nose and stared at it for a moment. "I think the bleeding has stopped."

A lock of hair had fallen over his forehead, and though she'd overheard him complaining to Kayla that he needed to get it cut and was asking for recommendations of where to do that, Maddie personally liked it. There was a vulnerability to him that she found quite attractive. She probably shouldn't be thinking such things about him, especially since he was hurt.

She couldn't deny that there was something

between them, not after the night at the Cattlemen's Ball, and certainly not now.

He gestured at the empty spot next to him. "Sit. I know you're supposed to watch me to make sure everything's okay, but I'd feel better if you weren't hovering over me."

Maddie shrugged as she joined him on the long padded bench they used as an examining table. "Occupational hazard," she said. "I'm not supposed to get so familiar with the patients, you know."

And, in spite of the very serious situation that was plaguing them, she gave a small, self-deprecating laugh. "As I'm sure you are well aware. Can you imagine the trouble I'd get into right now, cozying up to the patient like this?"

Luke scooted closer. "Well, if they talk, let's give them something to talk about." His voice was husky and warm, flowing over her body so gently and smoothly that it brought a warmth to her that she hadn't experienced in a long time.

"Now, now," she said. "I think you had a head injury, and it's affecting your judgment."

She hoped her tone was light and flirty, as she was trying to be. After all, she was out of practice with this flirting thing. They'd agreed to handle this. Maybe they should date like mature adults and talk about boundaries and how to handle it as a family at their next family therapy session.

Here she was, alone with Luke, and she couldn't deny the chemistry between them.

Luke must've been thinking the same thing, because he leaned forward, brushed a tendril of hair away from her face, and said, "Maddie, you are still the most beautiful woman I've ever seen. I know we said we need to figure this out as a family, but I want nothing more, right now, than to kiss you."

Even though the rational part of her brain told her she shouldn't, Maddie nodded. "I want that, too," she said.

As Luke leaned in closer, she leaned in to meet him, their lips joining in a tender embrace.

She couldn't remember the last time she'd been kissed by anyone like this, and she'd certainly never experienced anything so wonderful. As their lips came together, Maddie finally felt like she'd come home.

But just as briefly as their lips touched, footsteps sounded, and Kayla called out loudly, "Mom! Dad! Granny is riding a horse!"

They jumped apart, but not before Maddie realized that Kayla had seen them kissing.

Luke stood. "What do you mean Granny is riding a horse? We told her no. Everyone knew we didn't want Granny riding."

Maddie got to her feet, and they followed Kayla out.

"Yes," Maddie said. "We all agreed."

"I know." Kayla sounded annoyed. "One of the neighbors showed up with a puppy, and the twins went bonkers and ran after it. When everyone was busy chasing the twins, Granny climbed the steps next to where Stolley Bear was tied. And now she's riding him."

Of course, Granny took advantage of the moment. Because that's what Granny did. They should've watched her more carefully, or at least assigned someone to make sure she didn't go and do something stupid.

But when Maddie went to take care of Luke, how could they have predicted this?

"I'm sure she's fine," Luke said. "Everyone's watching her now, so we'll let her finish her ride, get her off the horse, and remind everyone of safety."

Maddie nodded. "As long as she doesn't get bucked off or something before we get there."

Kayla snorted. "When has Stolley Bear ever bucked?"

Maddie shrugged. "Well, never that I know of, but there's always a first time. Look at how everything is already not going according to plan."

Kayla gave her a sly grin. "You mean like you and Dad kissing?"

Oh boy. This was exactly what she didn't want to happen. That's why they had agreed that they were going to talk about this together as a family with a therapist before they did anything rash.

"That was a private moment between your mother and me," Luke said. "And while we are planning on having a family meeting with our counselor to make sure that we are all handling this appropriately, it doesn't give you the right to pry into our personal business. My relationship with your mom is my relationship with your mom. No meddling."

Maddie watched as Kayla gave a little sniff and flounced. "Fine by me. Just don't take so long about it. As Granny says, you two aren't getting any younger for getting me a sibling."

Maddie blanched at Kayla's words. What was Kayla thinking, making jokes like that? She was too angry to respond to her daughter, and held back. As Kayla ran ahead, Luke reached over and grabbed Maddie's hand. "It's okay," he said. "I know. We'll address that later together."

As they rounded the corner, Luke let go of her hand, as if by some unspoken agreement that even though Kayla had just caught them kissing, neither of them was ready to face their families' questions or Granny's eager gaze.

Besides, they had bigger fish to fry. As they got to the round pen, Granny was on the horse, grinning like a fool.

"Yeehaw," Granny shouted. She had one hand

on the reins, and one in the air like she was riding a bucking bronco, even though Stolley Bear was at a walk.

Even at her age, Granny still sat in the saddle in perfect form. Though it had been years since she'd been on a horse, her body remembered.

Brady was leading the horse, his hand on the reins by the horse's mouth so that even though Granny was holding the ends of the reins, he still had firm control. She also noticed that while they were trying not to make a big deal of it, Wyatt was walking along one side of the horse, constantly checking to make sure nothing went wrong.

Even though Maddie was concerned about Granny, and frustrated that Granny had gone against their instructions, at least everyone else had stepped up to make sure that Granny was safe.

Maddie opened the gate and entered the round pen. "Granny," she said. "Looks like you're riding a horse."

She kept her tone gentle but firm. She still hadn't figured out how to handle the situation. How do you chastise a grown woman for something like this? If Granny had been a child, Maddie knew exactly what she would say as she got the kid off the horse and gave her a stern talking-to about safety. But despite her extensive experience working with the elderly, Maddie had no words for this. The problem with how people like Briana treated Granny was that she was a grown woman, with a great deal of worldly experience, and she didn't need to be shamed like a child for her behavior. Oftentimes, the shame was what caused people like Granny to act out. So what did Maddie say here?

She glanced at Brady, who mouthed, "I'm sorry," and she understood. From what Kayla said, Granny had gotten on the horse when they'd all been distracted by the kids, so Brady had done the best he could to keep Granny from getting hurt.

Now the challenge was to get her off the horse just as safely.

Brady led the horse back to where they had been helping everyone get on and off, but then Granny started to cry. "Please. I'm not ready to get off."

Maddie went over to Granny and gently placed her hand on Granny's leg. "I know you don't want to, and I understand. But we need to get back to the house so everyone can eat."

At this point, making Granny feel bad about riding didn't seem like the right thing to do, especially since she didn't want to get off the horse. Maddie could always redirect Granny's attention for now, and later, when it was appropriate, they could have a conversation with Granny about the situation.

But as the men helped Granny off the horse, the older woman looked so heartbroken that Maddie sincerely felt bad. Though Stolley Bear had acted perfectly, and nothing had gone wrong, Granny had the stiff walk of someone who hadn't been on a horse in years. She'd be even worse tomorrow, which meant they'd have to come up with an explanation to keep Briana from crying foul.

Which was probably an exercise in futility, but hopefully they would get past it as they'd done with all of the other incidents involving Granny.

Even though Maddie genuinely prayed that Granny would be able to go home soon because Granny would be much happier there, it would also ease the sense of foreboding that followed Maddie around, making her wonder if the latest snag in the plans would be the one to finally cost her the job she'd been working so hard for.

Luke hated the brokenhearted expression on Granny's face as they helped her off the horse. He wished he could get her to understand that they were doing this out of love for her, not because they were trying to be mean to her.

His head throbbed from being kicked in the face, but at least the nosebleed had stopped. Who would've thought that giving a kid a piggyback ride would have caused so much trouble?

But when the toddler ran up to him and hugged his legs, saying, "I sowwy, Wuke," how could Luke be mad?

He ruffled Garrett's hair. "It's okay, buddy. Accidents happen."

Maddie caught his eye, and he returned her smile. They should probably treat this incident with Granny the same, but her actions were no accident.

Did she understand the risk she'd just taken?

Before following Maddie out of the round pen, Granny made another beeline back for the horse.

"Oh, Caramello," she said. "You're my best friend."

Then Granny wrapped her arms around the horse's neck, giving it a big hug.

Tears streamed down her face when she let go of the horse and turned back to them. "This has been the best day of my life," she said.

Then a mischievous grin filled her face. "Aside from the day that Gerald made me his bride."

Though he was concerned about his grandmother, and how they were going to deal with the fallout once Granny started telling everyone she'd ridden the horse, Luke couldn't help smiling at Granny's pronouncement. He could give all the excuses for why he hadn't married and settled down, but the truth was, no one had ever loved him like that, and he had never felt like that about anyone else.

As they started back to the house, Kayla ran up to Granny and put her arm around her. "Granny, that was fantastic. I can't wait until you're fully recovered and we can go on a trail ride together."

Then she looked over her shoulder at Luke and said, "Actually, I think we should all go on a family trail ride. After all, a former cavalry soldier is good with horses."

Luke laughed. "I keep telling you, they don't use horses for that purpose anymore. It's just ceremonial."

Kayla stuck her tongue out at him. "Yes, but I know you know how to ride a horse."

They had this discussion multiple times before, and while Luke eventually would go horseback riding with his daughter, it felt like a low priority compared to all the other things he needed to get done. Besides, it seemed incredibly unfair to go riding when Granny wasn't yet able to.

Still, he appreciated that everyone had kept the mood light after Granny's ride. Things had been tense for a while because they were all concerned for Granny's safety, but now that she was off the horse, everyone could breathe a little easier.

They could at least enjoy the rest of the day before heading back to reality and figuring out how they were going to keep Briana from blowing a gasket when Granny told her she'd ridden a horse.

When they got back to the house, they all gathered for the family meal, and Luke was grateful when Maddie sidled up to him and said, "Don't worry, everything here is allowed on Granny's diet. We specifically chose what she can eat because we didn't want to make her feel bad that she couldn't have what everyone else was having."

It was wrong of him to think so, but all he really wanted to do was pull Maddie back into his arms, hold her tight, and kiss her. The kiss they'd shared had only been a taste of what he hoped would be between them, and the deep level at which she loved his grandmother made her that much more attractive. But he caught Kayla's watchful eyes on him, as did Maddie. They stepped away.

"Who's hungry?" Maddie asked.

"Don't think I didn't just see that," Kayla said. "For two people I just caught kissing, you're bad liars about nothing going on between you two."

"That's enough," Luke said. "Didn't we just have this discussion? What's between me and your mother is none of your business right now."

Then he turned and looked at everyone in the room who was staring at him. Now that they knew about the kiss, they, too, seemed to think it solved everything between him and Maddie.

He'd felt guilty for not standing up for her before, so now was his chance.

"That goes for the lot of you," he said. "Look, I know you all mean well, but all this matchmaking is putting undue pressure on our relationship, and if you don't let things just happen naturally between the two of us, you're only going to drive us further apart."

He stole a glance at Maddie, to see if any of this was helping. He didn't want that first kiss to be their last. But he knew that if everyone kept pressuring them, it would only confirm all of Maddie's fears about the relationship. He'd been miserable when she was avoiding him, so the last thing he wanted was to push her away again.

"This chicken looks fantastic," Brady said.

Even though it was obvious to everyone that Brady was deliberately changing the subject, Luke appreciated it. He didn't want or need anyone else weighing in on this.

As Luke went to fill his plate, he saw Brady lean in and say something to Kayla, who stiffened like she was being chastised. Since Luke and Maddie had already had their words with Kayla, he hoped whatever Brady had to say would get through to her. But he also knew how he had been at that age.

Even though he'd followed in his father's footsteps by joining the army, he'd intentionally chosen a job that would take him as far away from his family as possible, putting him in danger. This made it clear to his father that while he was technically doing what his father wanted him to, he was going to do it his own way.

Certainly, he had his share of regrets over that decision, especially because it meant he'd missed out on watching his little girl grow up. But he also knew that his time in the army and the experiences he had had shaped him into the man he was today. He wasn't sure the young man he'd been when Kayla was conceived would have been that good of a father.

But his rebellion felt different from Kayla meddling in their lives. She didn't understand what was at stake.

When he got his plate and sat down next to Granny, she smiled at him. "I'm so glad you and Maddie are getting married," Granny said.

Great. This was why he should have been firmer in telling Kayla not to say anything about the kiss. Now that Granny knew, it was going to put so many big ideas in her head. How could he let her down?

"Granny, people kiss all the time, and they don't necessarily get married."

Saying it out loud made him feel like he was cheapening the experience he'd shared with Maddie.

But he couldn't express how much that one kiss meant to him. Not now, not in front of all these people who didn't understand. It was easy to play off their encounter all those years ago as just being a couple of drunk kids. But the truth was, he felt something for her then, and he felt something now.

But how was he supposed to explore those feelings with everyone trying to push them in a certain direction? As he looked at Granny's dejected face, he finally understood why Maddie was hesitant in getting involved with him.

What if they gave the relationship a chance, and for one reason or another, things just didn't work out?

He had dated enough women where that was the case. It wasn't that any of them had done anything wrong or they'd hurt one another, but there just wasn't that spark. Or the spark had faded over time.

Luke could see them going through the motions for longer than they needed to, simply because they didn't want to disappoint their families by telling them it was over. Even now, looking at the crushed expression on Granny's face made Luke's heart hurt.

How devastated would she be if, after a time, they'd been dating, and things ended? He looked over at Maddie, but she quickly turned away. Apparently, it was now too dangerous for them to even look at each other.

Like her husband, Josie seemed to understand the tension in the room and turned to Granny with a smile. "Ida Mae, I know that this is my second baby and all, but I was wondering if we could get together sometime and you could help me with my baby quilt? The ladies at church made a beautiful one for Shana, and I'd like this baby to have something as well."

Granny used to run the sewing circle at church, and she lit up at Josie's invitation. It was the perfect subject to distract Granny's attention, and Luke relaxed into his chair and joined in some of the other conversations happening at the table.

When he thought about his childhood and coming here to Granny's ranch, this was the sort of thing he remembered. Family gathered at the table, talking about a million different things, and sharing life together. He hated that he couldn't have that with Briana anymore. The times they'd gone over to her house, it was always stilted and uncomfortable, like Briana was still trying to punish Luke for his past and find evidence to keep him away from Granny.

Even though they had made strides in their relationship, Luke wondered if he and Briana would ever get beyond coexisting, and have a real relationship.

As they started clearing the plates, Granny looked around with a question on her face. "Where's Gerald? Has he gotten to eat yet?"

Everyone glanced around, their gazes landing on Maddie. After all, she was the expert in dealing with situations like this.

Luke's stomach knotted. Granny had never had a lapse in memory before. His grandfather had been dead for nearly ten years, so why was she asking for him now? They'd all been working so hard to get Granny home, thinking it was just a matter of her regaining physical strength. But what if it was something more?

"What do you mean, Granny?" Maddie asked.

Granny looked around the room again. "I can't believe that we had supper without Gerald. He's going to be mighty disappointed when he finds out that we ate without him."

Maddie smiled at Granny and held out her hand. "Why don't we have a seat in the living room and relax while we figure out what's going on?" Granny nodded, and as she got out of her chair to follow Maddie, she stopped and looked at Luke.

"Charles? Are you home? I thought you were at Fort Meade."

Luke swallowed the lump in his throat. Charles was his father, and he'd been stationed at Fort

Meade when Luke was so small he barely remembered that time.

"Granny, I'm Luke, Charles's son."

Granny gave him a strange look and shook her head. "I don't know what kind of game you're playing, but when I tell Gerald, you will all have a lot to answer for."

Maddie held her hand out to Granny again. "Come on, let's go to the living room. I think you'll be pleased to see how they've redecorated since you were here last. I'll let you get cozy on the sofa, and I'll bring you some coffee and dessert."

Instead of looking pleased at Maddie's offer, Granny frowned. "I should be helping with the dishes."

Maddie shook her head. "Oh, I wouldn't hear of it. In fact, young Kayla over there has volunteered to do all the cleanup today as part of a service project for her family to make up for sassing her parents."

At Kayla's groan, Luke bit back a laugh, in spite of his concern for Granny. He had to hand it to Maddie, she was one smart cookie who knew how to put her daughter in her place.

"Oh." Granny turned to Kayla. "I don't know who you are, young lady, but I suggest you start respecting your elders."

"But..." Kayla stared at Granny, obviously confused.

Granny put her hands on Kayla's shoulder and turned her toward the kitchen. Luke could tell by the expression on Kayla's face that she didn't understand why Granny just said that, but hopefully, in the kitchen, out of earshot of Granny, Brady could help their daughter.

Luke and Maddie got Granny settled with a slice of low-sugar apple crumble, and after chatting for a few moments, Granny dozed off.

When they finally took the empty dishes to the kitchen, Maddie said, "Granny fell asleep. But I think when she wakes up, we need to have her seen by a doctor. I know it's strange and scary that Granny is acting like she's in the past and doesn't remember things, but we need to be calm and loving toward her because if she sees us panicking, she's going to panic, too."

Kayla looked at her mom, a worried expression on her face. "She didn't know who I was."

Their daughter usually resisted her mom's hugs, but when Maddie opened her arms to Kayla, she ran right in and clung to her for dear life. "I know Granny's old, but I just got her."

Maddie squeezed her daughter tight. "It's going to be okay, I promise."

Maddie looked at everyone in the room and said, "It's unusual for a lapse of memory to come on this quickly. As we were in there talking, I tried to observe for signs of any other medical issue, and I don't think that's what's going on. But we'll let her rest, and then when she's ready, let the doctor give her an exam so that we can all make sure she's getting the best treatment possible."

Luke didn't know what he would've done if Granny had an episode like this and Maddie wasn't there. Once again, he was grateful for her, and he hoped that this latest setback wasn't going to create a deeper rift between them when Briana found out.

Even though his greatest concern was for Granny, he also knew that this was going to create even more issues with Briana. But he prayed that they could find a way to come together as a family to do what was best for Granny, as impossible as it seemed.

Chapter Nine

Maddie felt her heart pounding as she and Luke brought Granny through the emergency room, trying to maintain the air of calm she'd held since Granny had started acting strangely.

Even though Maddie had been reassuring everyone, the truth was, she was nervous, because Granny's sudden onset of forgetfulness wasn't normal, nor was it something she'd encountered before.

"Where am I?" Granny mumbled, her eyes wide and unfocused. "This isn't my house."

"Granny, it's okay. You're in the hospital," Maddie reassured her, trying to keep the fear from seeping into her voice. She knew how important it was for Granny to feel safe right now.

"Who are you people?" Granny asked, her gaze shifting between Maddie and Luke, a hint of panic flickering behind her blue eyes. "Oh. Charles. What are you doing home? Where is your father?"

Then a look of pained understanding filled

Granny's face. "Oh. Something's happened to Gerald, hasn't it?"

Maddie didn't know what was worse, Granny thinking they were at the hospital because something was wrong with her beloved husband, or that they would have to eventually tell her that he had died ten years ago.

This was a catastrophe.

"It's going to be okay," Maddie reassured Granny.

On the way to the hospital, Luke had texted Briana, and judging by the worried expression on his face, she was finally responding.

Maddie couldn't help but shiver as she watched the medical staff bustling around Granny, their faces etched with concern. They, too, were trying to act like everything was fine, giving Granny comfort and reassurance in her confusion. But Maddie's own training caught all the signs that this was a serious situation they weren't taking lightly.

She felt Luke's hand on her arm, offering a silent reassurance that they were in this together.

"Sir?" A nurse approached them, clipboard in hand. "We're going to need some information about your grandmother."

"Of course," Luke replied.

As the nurse scribbled down the answers, Maddie glanced back at Granny, who was now being wheeled away for more tests. Her heart ached at the sight of the elderly woman, so disoriented and vulnerable.

Maddie had already placed a call to Granny's social worker, and Eva came bustling through the doors.

"Did they already bring her back?" Eva asked.

"Yes," Maddie said. "Just through there, but I told them to expect you."

Even though it pained Maddie that she and Luke weren't by Granny's side in this moment, Granny didn't recognize Maddie, and she thought Luke was his late father. They would be less useful to Granny than the social worker, who would be able to document that everything had been done properly so Briana couldn't use any of this against them.

It felt incredibly unfair that this is what things had come to, but they had to keep their focus on the bigger picture, and what was best for Granny, and not just what they wanted.

"Thank you," Eva said, giving Maddie a warm smile before heading back to where they had Granny. They'd worked together on other cases, and Maddie knew that Eva's compassionate nature would help Granny.

Luke shifted in the chair next to her. "I hate that we have to sit here and do nothing. How long until you think they'll let us back there?"

Before Maddie could respond, Briana appeared at their side, her face a mask of barely contained fury. "What happened?" she demanded, her eyes darting between them. "Why is Granny here?"

"Granny got confused and disoriented," Maddie explained, trying to keep her voice steady. "We don't know what caused it yet, but they're running tests."

Briana crossed her arms, her gaze drifting from Maddie to Luke. "You'd better hope it's nothing serious," she told them coldly. "Because if anything happens to her while she's under your care, I'll make sure everyone knows it's your fault."

"Enough, Briana," Luke snapped, his anger flaring. "This isn't the time for your petty accusations. We're all worried about Granny here, so let's just focus on that."

"Fine," Briana huffed, taking a seat nearby, but not before shooting Luke one last venomous glare.

"Try to ignore her," Maddie whispered, reaching for Luke's hand and giving him a reassuring squeeze. "We need to stay strong for Granny, and that means sticking together."

Even though she could feel Briana's angry gaze on her drifting to the hand Maddie held, Maddie didn't let go. Luke needed her right now, even if that meant subjecting her to more of Briana's abuse.

Why did doing the right thing have to be so hard?

The warmth of Maddie's hand in his gave Luke more comfort than she could possibly know. It meant even more to him, feeling the weight of Briana's glare on them, suspecting she was judging Maddie, which Maddie was likely aware of as well.

After Maddie's confession about her insecurities over her reputation, Luke had promised himself to do whatever it took to protect her, even denying his own feelings.

It had to mean something that Maddie was willing to take this risk for him.

"Another health scare," Briana muttered under her breath, glaring at Luke and Maddie. "Always seems to happen when you two are around."

"Can we not do this right now?" Luke pleaded, trying to keep his voice level despite his rising frustration. "Granny needs our support, not petty arguments."

"Petty?" Briana scoffed, her gaze narrowing as she stood up and approached them. "I don't think it's petty to be concerned about my grandmother's well-being."

"Of course it isn't," Luke said, his tone even.

"We're all worried about Granny, Briana. That's why we brought her here—because we care about her. So let's save the family drama."

"Family drama?" Briana challenged, folding her arms across her chest. "Or are you deflecting so you have time to make up lies to cover up your wrongdoings?"

Luke's jaw clenched, and he tightened his grip on Maddie's hand. She gave him a squeeze back.

"Are you really suggesting that I'm deliberately harming Granny?" Luke asked, speaking quietly.

"You said it, not me," Briana snapped, her eyes glistening with unshed tears. "All I know is that my family's falling apart, and you're at the center of it."

Luke's heart ached as he looked at Briana—not just for himself and Maddie, but for the woman standing before them, consumed by jealousy and fear.

"Listen, Briana," he said softly, his voice gentle but firm. "We all want what's best for Granny, but tearing each other apart isn't going to help her. I'm sorry you feel like your family is falling apart. That's the last thing I wanted when I came home."

For once, Briana actually seemed like she was listening, so Luke took a deep breath and continued, "Please. Let's see what we're dealing with, and find out what's happening with Granny. Then we can figure out the best way to work together for Granny's sake."

Briana pursed her lips, looking unconvinced, but before she could respond, they were interrupted by the arrival of Granny's doctor.

"Good evening," he greeted them, his gaze moving between the three concerned faces. "I have an update about your grandmother's condition."

"Please," Luke urged, his voice wavering slightly. "Tell us what's going on with Granny."

The doctor nodded, taking a deep breath before he began. "Your grandmother has been diagnosed with transient global amnesia. It's a sudden, temporary episode of memory loss that can't be attributed to any known cause."

Luke's chest tightened at the news, his mind racing as he tried to process what this meant for Granny.

"Is it serious?" Briana asked, her voice barely audible as she clutched her hands together in her lap.

"Thankfully, it typically resolves itself within twenty-four hours, and most people who experience it have no lasting effects." the doctor replied, his tone reassuring. "However, we'd like to keep her here overnight for observation, just to be on the safe side."

Luke let out a soft sigh of relief, and he could feel Maddie's body relax beside him.

"Thank you, Doctor," Maddie said. "When can we see her?"

He smiled. "Soon. They're just getting her settled in a room, and then Eva will be down to talk to you all and bring you up."

As soon as the doctor left, Maddie squeezed his hand tight. "This is great news. I'm so glad Granny is going to be okay."

"Me too." Luke wanted to pull her in his arms, but he knew he was already pushing Maddie's boundaries with the hand-holding.

Briana, however, didn't seem to share their optimism. Her face twisted into a scowl as she glared at Maddie and Luke, her eyes dark with accusation. "If you two hadn't been so focused on playing house, this never would have happened," she spat, her voice trembling with anger.

"Excuse me?" Maddie replied indignantly, taking her hand out of Luke's.

"Granny needed us, and we were there for her," Luke shot back, his voice firm yet controlled. He wasn't about to let Briana's misplaced anger get the better of him.

"Really?" Briana sneered. "Because it seems like every time she's left alone with you two, something goes wrong. What exactly do you two do when you're at the stables? Are you really watching Granny?"

Luke's gut twisted at the accusation. He'd never admit it to Briana, but this time at least, Granny had gotten into trouble when their backs had been turned. But it hadn't been nearly as sordid as Briana was making it out to be.

"Transient global amnesia isn't caused by anyone, Briana," Maddie interjected, looking like she was doing her best to remain calm despite the hurtful accusations being thrown their way. "The doctor explained that there isn't any known cause. Based on what I know of it, the medical community doesn't have any clear answers as to why it happens."

"If you know so much," Briana said, her tone sharp and biting, "then why did you bring her into the emergency room?"

Eva joined their group. "Because the symptoms Ida Mae presented could have been a number of things, and Maddie was wise to seek medical attention to rule out anything more serious."

Though Maddie appreciated Eva's defense, it didn't take the scowl off of Briana's face.

"And why were you called in? If they have nothing to hide, why was your presence necessary?"

The expression on Eva's face didn't change as she said, "Precisely for this reason. You're questioning the care Ida Mae received under Luke and Maddie's supervision, and I'm here to make sure that everything was done properly, which it was. Remember, I'm here as an advocate for Ida Mae. Your interests are immaterial to me, because my responsibility is to her."

It would have been completely inappropriate for Luke to do a fist pump at this point, but he wanted to. What was it going to take for Briana to understand that their focus should be on Granny?

"Anyway," Eva said, "Ida Mae is resting right now, and while I'm happy for all of you to go see her, I really must caution you against upsetting her. She still doesn't remember what's going on, so please be gentle and don't force any issues with her. If you must continue your family squabbles, please do so outside of her presence."

Luke felt bad that he was part of the family squabble even though he had been doing his best to avoid it.

Eva gave them the information for Granny's room, and when Luke, Maddie, and Briana were alone in the elevator, Briana said, "There might not be a known cause, but it sure is convenient that it happened when you two were in charge."

Luke clenched his jaw, trying to swallow the angry retort that threatened to spill out. He knew that arguing with Briana would only make matters worse, but it was difficult to hold his tongue when faced with such baseless accusations.

"Enough," Luke said firmly, his voice cutting through the tension like a knife. "We all love Granny, and right now, playing the blame game isn't helping."

"Fine," Briana muttered, crossing her arms tightly over her chest. "But don't think for a second that I'm going to let you two off the hook."

When they got to Granny's room, she was asleep, snoring softly. She looked so peaceful, and Luke was hopeful that tomorrow, things would seem better.

If only resolving things with Briana would come as easy.

The flickering fluorescent light above them cast an eerie glow as Briana's gaze bore into him, her voice low and cold. "I don't think either of you is capable of taking care of Granny properly. She's had too many coincidental mishaps."

"All easily explainable," Luke said. They stepped out into the hall, and he tried to remain calm as he closed Granny's door firmly behind them. Eva asked them to not fight in front of Granny, and the last thing he wanted was for her to wake up to them arguing.

"I don't want to hear your excuses," Briana said, her voice dripping with venom. "It's clear that no one here is taking my concerns about

Granny seriously, so I'm looking into having Granny transferred to a facility in Denver. Maybe there she'll receive better care and be away from your influence."

Briana's eyes were filled with conviction, making it clear that she was serious about her intentions.

"Granny is family, Briana," Luke said, his voice strained as he tried to maintain control of his emotions. "We love her and want what's best for her. Taking her away from her home and everyone she knows isn't the answer. Her house is almost ready. Maybe you and Corey could come by sometime and help with the final details."

"Granny isn't capable of living on her own," Briana said, her tone sharp as a knife. "You haven't been here like I have. I tried helping her, but she wouldn't let me. I'm sure you looked at the house and thought we must be neglecting her. That's far from the truth, and you'd know it if you'd have been here."

Tears rolled down Briana's face, and for the first time, it hit him how hard this must all be on her. He'd been so focused on Granny that he hadn't given much thought to what it had been like for Briana.

"You're right," he said softly. "I'm sorry. Since Granny is sleeping, let's go get some coffee or something, and we can talk. For real this time."

Briana shook her head. "It's too little, too late. I'll be talking to the place in Denver to see how soon they can get her in. This was the last straw."

Luke watched as Briana stormed away, her heels clicking angrily on the hospital floor.

"Luke," Maddie said softly, placing her hand on his arm. "What are you thinking?"

He sighed, running a hand through his short-cropped hair. "I'm worried about Granny, obviously," he admitted, his voice strained. "But I'm also… I can't help but wonder if maybe Briana has a point."

Maddie stared at him. "You don't really think we're hurting Granny, do you?"

"No, of course not," Luke replied quickly, reaching out to take Maddie's hand. "Maybe it would be better for Granny to be at a facility without any personal connection to us. That way, there would be no bias in her care, and your job wouldn't be at risk."

Then he sighed, not wanting to face the truth. "Maybe we're being too optimistic that Granny can come home. People who don't know her might do a better job of evaluating her readiness."

"I don't believe that for a second," Maddie said. "No offense to Briana, but she's too harsh with Granny. I know Briana means well. But she treats Granny like a child instead of a full-grown adult. We just all need to find a way to work together."

Did Maddie realize that she'd just said "we" in terms of working together?

Luke probably shouldn't be thinking these thoughts, even though their kiss today had given him more hope for their future than he'd had since discovering their connection. But it felt good to realize that even with Briana's attacks, Maddie wasn't pulling away from him.

Still, would it be enough to fix all the things falling apart around them?

Chapter Ten

Maddie stepped into Granny's hospital room, the delicate scent of herbal tea wafting from the travel mug she carefully carried in one hand. In her other hand was a container of freshly baked muffins, made with ingredients that adhered to Granny's strict dietary requirements.

Granny was sitting in her bed, looking as she always did when Maddie checked in on her the mornings she was at the senior center. It was hard to believe she'd spent the night in the hospital, except for all the equipment monitoring her condition.

"Good morning, Granny," Maddie said gently, setting the items on the small table beside the hospital bed. "I know hospital food is worse than what you get at the senior center, so I brought you a little treat."

A twinkle shone in her eyes. "I suppose they're made with the healthy garbage you like. You didn't put kale in it, did you?"

Maddie laughed. "No kale, I promise. Just lots

of healthy super fruits and all sorts of yummy goodness."

She opened the container and held a muffin out to Granny, who sniffed it suspiciously. "Is there chocolate in it?"

"What do you think?" Maddie asked, grinning.

Despite her concerns, Granny took a bite. "Hey, this isn't bad!"

"Now have some tea," Maddie urged. "It's the blend I bring you at the senior center. No caffeine, so I know you can have it."

Granny frowned. "Yeah, they said I couldn't have coffee. I really wanted a cup."

Maddie took a deep breath. Though Granny was in the hospital because of her amnesia episode, the doctors had found some concerning things in her blood work. "I know. And we need to talk about that, because it seems to me that someone isn't sticking to her diet."

Giving an exaggerated sigh, Granny said, "Even the Bible says people need salt."

Great. Now Maddie was going to have to debate the theology of nutrition with Granny. The old woman knew her Bible better than anyone else Maddie was acquainted with, so the last thing she wanted was to get into this discussion.

"Not in excess," Maddie said. "Your blood work shows it's been in excess. What I don't understand is that with the care we're taking to monitor your diet, how are you getting all this sodium? When we get you back to the center, we'll schedule an appointment with your doctor to find out what's going on."

Thankfully, Granny didn't look like she wanted to argue further, mostly because she knew she'd been caught. Maddie wasn't naive enough to believe that Granny hadn't been getting secret treats somehow, because there was no other reason for her levels to change so drastically.

"These muffins are so delicious," Granny said, taking another bite.

Busted.

"See? Healthy food doesn't have to taste bad," Maddie said.

Granny swallowed, still looking cranky. "It could have used more sugar."

Maddie shook her head. "You're impossible. I just wish you could understand that we're trying to get you home. We're not being mean for the sake of torturing you. This is for your own good."

"Speaking of home," Granny said, wiping a crumb from her mouth, "I feel so much better now. When can I go back?"

Glancing at the open door, Maddie said, "As soon as the doctor comes in and gives you a final all-clear, we'll bring you back to the senior center."

"I don't know what all this fuss is about,"

Granny said. "I still don't understand why I'm even here."

Maddie hesitated for a moment, not wanting to upset Granny with the details of the previous day. "You don't remember what happened yesterday, do you?"

Granny shook her head, her brow furrowing in confusion. "No. But I think there was a barbecue at the stables." The furrow in her brow got even deeper. "Why can't I remember? What happened yesterday?"

They hadn't talked about how they were going to tell Granny about the previous day. But the worry on Granny's face made Maddie feel like she ought to say something.

"There was a lot of excitement for you yesterday at the stables."

Before Maddie could answer, Kayla came bounding in the room.

"Granny! Are you feeling better?"

"I'd be better if I was sleeping in my own bed, instead of having these people wake me up every time I got into the dream zone."

Kayla gave a perfect teenager groan. "I hate that. My alarm does that to me every morning."

Granny made a face. "This is worse than an alarm. I still don't understand why everyone is making such a fuss."

"You were acting really funny yesterday,

Granny," Kayla said, plopping into the chair next to the bed. "You didn't even know who I was."

Maddie wished she could take the expression of pain from Granny's face.

"What else happened yesterday?" Granny asked.

Kayla's face lit up. "You rode Stolley Bear!" Then she frowned. "But you weren't supposed to, and Mom and Dad were really upset with you."

"Did I really?" Granny asked, her voice filled with surprise.

Maddie nodded, swallowing the lump in her throat. "Yes, but you shouldn't have, and we were all worried about you. Then you started talking like we were in the past, so we thought it best to bring you here. Did the doctor explain any of this to you?"

Granny's face fell, and she looked down at her hands, clearly saddened by Maddie's words. "He said something about some kind of temporary amnesia. I'm sorry for causing everyone so much trouble. I wish I could remember it, though."

Then she looked over at Kayla. "Especially the part about riding Stolley Bear. That must have been something!"

"Oh, it was," Kayla said, the grin returning to her face. "I took some videos if you want to see."

Maddie didn't really want to relive the day, and she needed to have a word with the nurses anyway.

"Okay, you two. I'm going to go talk to the nurses, so I'll let Kayla show you the videos. Just remember that you weren't supposed to be riding Stolley Bear, and we're not letting you do it again until the doctor says it's okay."

Kayla sighed, taking Granny's hand in hers and giving it a reassuring squeeze. "You did really good, Granny. But everyone was upset because you could have gotten hurt. Once the doctor says it's okay, though, I promise to take you on an even better ride. We'll go as a family."

The tears in Granny's eyes made Maddie's heart melt. Even though everything was so messed up right now, she couldn't regret the relationship she'd given both Maddie and Granny.

"Thank you, Kayla," Granny said. "That means the world to me."

Maddie stepped out, giving them some alone time to share their moment, and went in search of the nurse in charge of Granny's case. It was unusual that Briana hadn't shown up yet, but it was also nice to have a break.

At the nurses' station, Maddie saw that the person she needed to speak to was on the phone, so she patiently waited for her to finish. It was strange, being on the other end of the care continuum, but it was a good reminder on how to have empathy for her patients and their families. And as she was kept waiting longer than she would have liked, it felt good to have patience for the harried woman who was just trying to do her job at what seemed like an extremely busy time.

Once she talked to the nurse about getting Granny's discharge instructions and coordinating with the senior center, she went back to Granny's room. Granny and Kayla were giggling together like schoolgirls, their heads close as they whispered something that Maddie couldn't quite make out. The sight warmed her heart, and she couldn't help but smile as she approached them.

"All right, ladies," she said playfully, "What's going on? What am I missing here?"

"Ah, Maddie," Granny said, still giggling as she wiped away a tear. "It's just a little secret between me and Kayla here."

Kayla nodded in agreement, her eyes dancing with mischief. "Yep, just us girls, Mom."

"I see how it is," Maddie teased, feigning offense. "I'll remember this the next time I have a secret." She winked at them both, happy to see their spirits lifted.

"Anyway," Kayla said, standing up and smoothing her skirt. "I've got to go. I promised Dad and Josie I'd come over for a bit today." She leaned down to Granny for a quick peck on the cheek and then gave Maddie her usual wave before heading out.

"Okay, Granny," Maddie said, settling into the

chair next to Granny's bed. "Now that it's just us, are you going to tell me what all the giggling was about?"

"Nice try, Maddie," Granny replied, chuckling softly. "But a secret's a secret. You'll just have to wait and see what it's about."

"Fine," Maddie said. "I talked to the nurse, and they're working on the paperwork to get you back to the senior center and to coordinate the doctor information."

"I thought my amnesia was temporary," Granny said, looking worried.

Maddie took Granny's hand. "It was. But they are worried about the results of your blood work, and the doctors are talking to see what we're going to do moving forward. Honestly, I'm kind of glad this happened, because they did a lot of tests to see what's going on. Now we know that you're not sticking to your diet, so the doctors need to determine the next plan of action."

As Maddie talked, Granny looked more downcast. "You're really mad at me, aren't you?"

Maddie shrugged. "As I've been telling everyone, you're a grown woman who can make decisions for herself. I just wish you'd understand that no one is trying to be mean to you. We all love you and want the best for you, so somehow we've got to figure out a way to make this work for everyone."

Granny nodded slowly, like she understood what Maddie was saying and didn't like it. But it was up to Granny to make the decision about her health. Maddie couldn't do it for her.

"I'll try to do better," Granny said, patting her hand affectionately. Then her eyes twinkled with mischief, and she raised an eyebrow. "But speaking of secrets… Kayla did tell me about something else."

"Oh?" Maddie asked, knowing Granny was trying to change the subject. She'd let her, because Granny was likely to get a very stern talking-to from Briana, and she didn't want to add to Granny's stress.

"Indeed," Granny continued, a teasing smile playing at the corners of her mouth. "She mentioned something about you and Luke sharing a little…kiss?"

Maddie felt her face heat, and she looked away, unable to meet Granny's gaze. She'd definitely be having words with Kayla later.

"Oh, that," she mumbled, wishing she had a better answer. "It was just a mistake."

"A mistake?" Granny echoed, her smile fading as she regarded Maddie with concern. "Why do you say that?"

"Because…" Maddie began, struggling to find the right words. "That moment took our focus off of what was important. We should have been making sure you were safe and shielding Kayla from any potential disappointment. Instead, we let ourselves get caught up in our own emotions."

Granny listened silently for a moment, her expression thoughtful as she squeezed Maddie's hand reassuringly. "My dear," she started gently, "you are allowed to have moments of happiness, too. You don't always have to put everyone else first."

The others had been telling her that as well, but they didn't understand what Maddie's mistakes had cost her. She didn't regret having Kayla for a second, but no one understood what it was like to be under constant scrutiny for having made that mistake.

"Granny, I appreciate your concern," Maddie said softly. "But I've made so many mistakes in my life that I need to be sure no one else is harmed by my actions. If that means giving up a chance at romance with Luke, then that's a sacrifice I'm willing to make."

"You're too hard on yourself," Granny replied, her voice firm but gentle. "You can't keep everyone safe all the time. I'm a grown woman, and while I don't remember what happened yesterday, looking after me isn't your responsibility. And Kayla is practically an adult. You need to trust that she can handle herself."

Hadn't everyone else been telling her the same thing?

And yet, because Maddie had that private moment with Luke, Granny had gotten on the horse. While they couldn't say what had caused Granny's amnesia, Maddie had read enough about it to see that one of the suspected causes was the person having a highly emotional experience.

Riding Stolley Bear was definitely a highly emotional experience. Had Maddie's momentary lapse caused Granny's setback?

Maddie sighed, staring down at her fingers intertwined with Granny's. "I know, and I'm trying. It's just not as simple as everyone seems to think."

"Sometimes, letting go and trusting in others is the best way to show your love," Granny advised, her eyes warm and understanding. "And perhaps, in allowing yourself a chance at happiness with Luke, you'll find that your love for each other can only strengthen the bonds between all of us."

Maddie considered Granny's words, feeling a mixture of hope and fear tug at her heart. Could she really allow herself to be with Luke, without risking harm to those she cared about?

Maybe, but the middle of a family crisis and so close to Kayla finishing school wasn't the time to test that theory. Once Kayla was settled in college, and Granny was thriving back at home, then she could consider it.

"Close your eyes, dear," Granny instructed

softly. Maddie hesitated for a moment, then complied. She felt Granny gently sliding rings onto Maddie's fingers, one by one. The rings fit perfectly, as if they had been made just for her. Maddie opened her eyes in surprise, looking down at the golden bands now adorning her hand.

"Granny, what are you doing?" she asked, her voice barely above a whisper.

"Those rings were blessed by the Lord when Gerald and I exchanged our vows," Granny explained quietly, her gaze locked on Maddie's hand. "And I believe, with all my heart, that you and Luke are meant to be together. Someday, those rings will be yours."

Maddie stared at the rings, feeling their weight on her fingers, and the significance of Granny's gesture weighed heavily on her heart.

Maddie looked into Granny's eyes, seeing the love and conviction that filled them. But as much as she appreciated Granny's faith in her and Luke, she couldn't bring herself to let Granny think they had a future.

"Granny," Maddie said softly, taking off the rings and placing them back into Granny's hand. "I'm so grateful for your love and support, but you can't promise these to me. They belong to you, and they're a symbol of the beautiful life you and Gerald shared."

She closed Granny's fingers around the rings,

feeling the warmth of their connection through their touch. "Luke and I are just friends, and that's how it has to be. I know your heart is in the right place, but I need you to accept my decision."

Granny studied Maddie's face for a moment, her expression thoughtful. Finally, she sighed and nodded. "Fine. I won't push you anymore. But promise me one thing."

"Anything, Granny," Maddie replied, her voice laced with relief.

Granny's eyes bore deep into Maddie, almost desperately. "Please don't write off being with Luke simply because you're afraid of what others think. You have to stop living your life chasing after the good opinion of other people. The ones who matter will love you no matter what."

Hadn't Maddie and Luke had a similar conversation at the Cattleman's Ball? It felt like a lifetime ago.

Back when Maddie's scandals erupted, it felt like the world was closing in on her, with no one there to support her. Could it be different this time?

Maybe.

But Maddie also wasn't sure she had the strength to face having her life fall apart again.

Luke wandered the empty stables, looking for Kayla. She'd left her bag in his SUV the other day when they'd taken Granny to the hospital, and she'd asked him to meet her here so she could get it back.

Maddie came around the corner, then stopped when she saw him. "Hey. What are you doing here? Kayla doesn't ride today."

Holding up the bag, Luke said, "I was given the impression that Kayla needed this urgently."

"Right." Maddie groaned. "Even though she agreed to back off on the thought of our romance after witnessing our kiss, I think she's still trying to play matchmaker. She knew I was coming over here to drop off some of the things the sewing circle made."

Luke sighed, shaking his head. "I should've known she was up to something when she asked if I was busy and then said she needed her bag. Why hasn't she needed it sooner?"

Then he chuckled in spite of the situation. "You and Brady warned me that she could be sneaky. I guess it was my turn to be on the receiving end."

Maddie's warm laugh filled him with peace. It was the sound of two people who were in it together.

"I know we didn't really talk about the kiss, or us, since everything got so chaotic that day," Luke said, hating the words that were going to come next, but feeling like he had to say them.

Shrugging, Maddie said, "We have way more

important things to worry about than a poorly timed kiss. Don't stress about it."

She'd just put everything he'd been feeling into words, and yet it felt empty hearing them from her. Part of him wished she cared enough about him to fight for their relationship, but logic told him that she was also right about it being bad timing.

After all, had it not been for them getting distracted, Granny wouldn't have gotten on that horse, and maybe this whole thing wouldn't have happened.

Because it wasn't just about the kiss. It was about how he'd spent that whole day, mooning over Maddie, falling in love with her family, and being grateful to be part of it. The Shepherd's Creek family was everything he'd always wanted in a family, but he hadn't known he'd wanted it until he'd gotten to experience it.

The little boy had kicked Luke in the face because Luke was too busy staring at Maddie like a lovesick teenager. He hadn't been paying attention.

Which led to Granny riding the horse, then having her amnesia episode, and everything falling apart with Briana.

As soon as Briana found out that Granny had gotten on a horse, even though they had plenty of people to back Luke and Maddie up about it being

Granny's choice to break the rules, it gave Briana reason to move Granny to a facility in Denver, where it would be harder to take Granny out on excursions like what had happened the other day.

"You're right," Luke finally told Maddie. "We don't need the distraction in our lives right now."

At least she looked as pained to hear it as it felt to say it.

"Maybe someday," Maddie said. "I know Kayla wants us to be together more than anything, but I don't think she realizes how much it's costing us."

"What is wrong with you people?" Kayla demanded, stepping out from one of the stalls. "You have the kind of true love that's better than any movie, and even though everyone is telling you to be together, you're making a bunch of dumb excuses."

Was this what Maddie had to live with constantly?

"I don't like your tone of voice," Luke said. "This is beyond disrespectful. We're trying to do the right thing here, and it's not your place to interfere or judge."

Instead of backing down, Kayla squared her shoulders. "The right thing is to be there for your daughter as a family. This is all I've wanted my whole life, and you're both being too stubborn to be good parents."

Whoa. Maddie looked like Kayla had just slapped her, and the gut punch was nothing like what Luke had expected.

"You're a child. You don't know anything about being good parents," he said.

"Mom was my age when she had me," Kayla retorted. "And I make way better choices than the two of you did."

Before Luke could process Kayla's hurtful comments, Kayla turned and looked at her mother. "You tell everyone you do all this stuff for me, but when it comes down to it, you're really just selfish. You don't care about what I need at all."

Maddie had looked like she'd been slapped in the face before, but now her expression turned to anguish, like she'd been stabbed in the gut.

Luke glared at Kayla. His daughter or no, Maddie didn't deserve this. "Don't talk to your mother like that."

"I'm technically an adult. I can say what I want." Kayla put her hands on her hips, trying to look tough, but Luke could see her for the scared little girl that she was.

"Maybe in age," Luke said quietly. "But you've still got a lot of maturing to do before I'll consider you an adult. You're acting like a child, and this needs to stop."

He stole a glance at Maddie, who looked like

she was doing everything she could to hold it together. She'd lived with the shame of her actions for so long, and now her own daughter was judging her. No wonder she'd been fighting their attraction. If only Luke had done a better job doing the same.

"You barely came back into my life, so you have no right to tell me anything."

Maddie took a step forward. "Enough. Kayla, this level of disrespect is completely unacceptable. I don't care how old you are. You don't get to talk to people like this."

"Fine," Kayla said, glaring at them both. "I'm going to my real dad's, where I know he actually cares about what I want. It's his day anyway, so you can't stop me."

Turning on her heel, Kayla stomped off.

Even though Kayla was right about Luke barely being back in her life, it didn't stop the deep pain in Luke's heart at hearing Brady referred to as Kayla's real dad. Until now, he hadn't realized how much it hurt to know how he hadn't been there for his little girl.

Maddie stepped beside him and took his hand. "I know. It hurts. I've been through this before with her, only in that case, I was in the wrong. We're not wrong here, and Kayla has to learn to accept that when it comes to other people's hearts, it's not her place to dictate."

Even though he'd been telling himself all this time that he didn't need Maddie, her hand in his was the only thing keeping him steady right now.

"But I hurt her," he said quietly.

Maddie squeezed his hand. "We've been telling her all along that this wasn't happening. Maybe she'll finally see the truth."

Was it the truth? Yes, they'd agreed not to have a relationship, but if they were talking about the truth here, Luke *did* want a relationship with Maddie. He just didn't want to pay the price of losing everything else.

He closed his eyes as he realized this was how Maddie had been living ever since she'd found out she was pregnant. All along, he'd felt bad about the sacrifices she'd made, giving up her own personal happiness for Kayla's sake.

But as Maddie had been saying all along, things were way more complicated than simply being willing to give their relationship a try.

God, please help us. I've only been a parent for a couple of months, and I'm clearly not doing it right. I've lost the woman I love, and I'm not doing a great job of helping my grandmother or my daughter. Show me the way, because I don't know what else to do.

Chapter Eleven

Maddie surveyed the activity in Granny's room as Luke and Briana were working to pack things up. Things had been tense in the week that followed their confrontation in the barn with Kayla, and Kayla was still not speaking to her. Their family therapist had encouraged Maddie to give Kayla some space, so Maddie was doing her best to respect that.

The past week had been harder than Maddie could have imagined. This had been the longest Maddie had gone without spending time with her daughter, and she'd been missing Luke as well.

Worse, Briana had convinced Luke and Granny that the best place for Granny was some nursing home in Denver.

As Maddie stole a glance at Luke, he seemed like a shell of the man she'd first met when he'd come here. Part of her wanted to pull him aside and ask him what he'd been thinking, but with the way Briana kept glancing in Maddie's direction, Maddie didn't dare.

When Claire had stoically informed Maddie of Granny's decision to move, it had come with the subtle reminder that Maddie needed to stay out of the situation. All Maddie had to do was get through today without incident, and tomorrow, she'd have her final interview with the board of directors about taking Claire's place.

Easy peasy.

Except none of it felt like a victory.

In fact, Maddie felt sick to her stomach, watching what felt like a travesty.

No one in the room, save Briana, looked happy.

Kayla entered the room, then stopped short as her eyes lit on Maddie, then on Luke. Brady had told Maddie that he'd spoken with Kayla and said she was being unreasonable and needed to apologize, but so far, not a peep.

"I can't believe you're really moving. This is so unfair," Kayla said, obviously having learned nothing about not being so blunt. But at least she'd said what everyone besides Briana had been thinking.

Granny looked at Kayla sadly. "I know, but maybe it'll finally stop all the fighting."

Would it?

Maddie had her doubts, but it wasn't her place to say so. That's why they had the social worker advocating for Granny, and somehow Eva had agreed to it.

Briana walked over to the small table where they kept Granny's teas and other treats. As she started putting the things in a box, she lifted the bowl of spices Luke had made. "I'm not sure what to do with this. It's going to spill in the box."

She held up the bowl and dipped a finger in it. "What's in it, anyway?"

As quickly as Briana put her finger in her mouth, she made a face. "Salt! What is the meaning of this? I thought we were controlling your salt. No wonder your blood work was so bad."

"That's not possible," Luke said, taking the bowl from Briana, then tasting it himself. He also made a face.

"Granny! What happened to the spice mixture I made you?"

Instead of backing Luke up, Briana glared at him. "Nice fake surprise. I should have looked into this sooner."

Things might not be good between Luke and Maddie, but Maddie believed him. He looked genuinely distressed that what he'd been trying to help Granny with had become something that had harmed her. And this was causing yet another conflict with Briana.

"Oh, stop, you harpy," Granny said. "Luke's mixture didn't have any salt. I added some to give it more flavor. You can't control everything I do."

Maddie bit back the urge to laugh. Though

Briana had won this round, Granny wasn't going down without a fight. And at least Granny had defended Luke. Not that Briana looked like she believed it.

"You'll say anything to protect him. Just like all those times he caused trouble as a teenager. You let him get away with it then, and you're letting him get away with it now."

The fury on Briana's face was evident, and Maddie said a silent prayer that God would help Briana find comfort and forgiveness. The bitterness she was carrying over a grudge that was nearly twenty years old was tearing her family apart, and Briana needed the hand of God more than anything to help her.

"What do you want from me?" Luke asked. "How long do you need me to pay for my sins before they're forgiven?"

Then he gestured at Maddie. "How long does she need to pay?"

Maddie shrank back, trying not to be part of this. She was too close to getting what she'd dreamed of to have it ruined now.

Luke returned his attention to Briana. "We go to the same church. Tell me where it says in the Bible how long we are to be punished before our sins can be let go of?"

Even though it was a mostly rhetorical question, Maddie had hoped Briana would give some kind of answer. Instead, Briana put a few more things into the box she'd been packing.

"Granny's stuff isn't going to pack itself."

Maybe Luke's speech didn't have an impact on Briana, but Kayla had stepped closer to Maddie, almost to the point of touching. At least Kayla was taking Luke's words to heart.

Briana picked up the small box Granny kept her rings in, and frowned. Then she opened the lid.

"Granny? Where are your rings?"

Granny looked puzzled. "They should be in the box. My fingers have been swollen lately, so I put them away."

The expression on Briana's face darkened. "They're not here."

A hush fell over the room as everyone looked up in shock. Granny frowned, her eyes searching the room for any sign of the missing belongings.

"I know I put them in the box," Granny said.

"What about on your nightstand by your lotion?" Maddie suggested. "I know you often set them there when you put on your hand cream."

As she spoke, she looked over at the empty nightstand. It had already been cleared of Granny's belongings.

"You seem to know an awful lot about Granny's rings," Briana said. "I saw you in the hospital, trying them on. Though you gave them back to Granny, perhaps you wanted them for yourself, after all. You probably didn't think anyone would notice them missing in the bustle of the packing."

Maddie's heart dropped as she felt the weight of Briana's accusation. She could feel the eyes of everyone in the room on her, their gazes filled with varying degrees of shock and disbelief.

"Briana, you've misunderstood what happened..." Maddie began, but her voice trailed off as she realized that defending herself would be an uphill battle against Briana's determination to discredit her.

She didn't take the rings, so she had nothing to worry about. But they had to find them, and fast, to ease the sting of Briana's accusation.

"Maddie would never take my rings." Granny said. Her eyes filled with love and concern. "It's true I gave them to her in the hospital to try on, but she wouldn't accept them, even though I still want her to have them."

Granny's defense of her only lifted Maddie's spirits slightly. Briana was looking at Maddie like she'd committed an unpardonable sin, and both Luke and Kayla wore expressions Maddie couldn't read.

"Let's just clear this up right now," Briana said, her voice dripping with false sweetness. "If you didn't take them, then you have no problem showing us what's in your bag."

That gave Maddie an even greater sense of security. Her bag was safely in her locker in the employee break room. There was no way Granny's rings would be there.

"I believe we need Claire to witness this," Briana said, pulling out her cell phone. Claire had given Briana her cell phone number because it was wearing thin on the staff to constantly call her in response to Briana's demands.

When Claire arrived, Briana explained the situation to her. Even though Maddie could see the doubt and frustration in Claire's eyes, Maddie knew that Claire had to follow policy.

"We'll have security go with Maddie to her locker, and we can look at things there."

"No," Briana said stiffly. "I want her to bring them here so we can all see for ourselves that she's a lying thief."

"I have nothing to be afraid of," Maddie said. "We can get my things and search them here."

Though it was humiliating for Maddie to let Claire call security, then have them walk her to her locker to get her bag, she held her head high, knowing she did nothing wrong.

When they got back to the room, Maddie handed her bag to Claire, trying to maintain her composure as her boss searched through the contents.

A heavy silence settled over the room, punctuated only by the sounds of items being moved around in the bag. The tension was palpable, each second feeling like an eternity. And then, Claire's eyes widened as she pulled something out of Maddie's bag.

"Is this what you're looking for?" Claire asked, holding up the rings, her voice a mixture of disappointment and disbelief.

Maddie stared at the rings in shock, unable to comprehend how they had ended up in her possession. Her mouth opened and closed, but no words came forth. Her heart ached, knowing that the people she cared about most now questioned her integrity.

"Maddie, I'm sorry to have to do this," Claire said softly, her voice laced with sadness. "You're fired."

The room spun as Claire's words echoed in Maddie's head. *Fired.*

"Wait, this isn't right!" Maddie exclaimed, her voice cracking with emotion as she stared at the rings in Claire's hand. "I didn't take those. I would never do that!"

Her eyes welled up with tears, and she desperately tried to blink them away. It was hard enough having her integrity questioned, but the thought of losing everything she had worked so hard for was almost unbearable.

She looked over at Luke, but he wouldn't meet her gaze.

As she glanced around the room at the shocked expressions, Maddie realized that she had zero support. How could she, when the rings had been found in her possession?

Briana looked satisfied, at least. This is what the other woman had wanted all along, so why shouldn't she be happy?

Even though Maddie hated for her daughter to witness this, she turned to Kayla. She was never going to forgive Maddie now.

"Mom didn't take those rings!" Kayla said, stepping forward. Her gaze locked onto Briana, a fire smoldering in her eyes. "You did it, didn't you, Briana? You're just trying to sabotage my mom's relationship with Luke and Granny!"

Briana rolled her eyes at the accusation. "Why on earth would I do something like that?"

It was obvious Briana had something to do with the rings being in Maddie's bag. But Maddie had no way of proving it. Nor did she know how the rings would have ended up in her bag.

Granny, who had worn an unreadable expression on her face, finally spoke up.

"Everyone, please," she said, raising her hands to quiet the room. "Let's try to find a reasonable explanation for all this. I know Maddie, and I can't believe she would do something like this.

If she'd wanted the rings, all she had to do was ask. I'd already offered them to her."

Maddie felt her heart swell with gratitude for Granny's unwavering faith in her, even in the face of the evidence. But she could see the doubt in Luke's eyes.

"See?" Kayla said. "Mom didn't have to steal anything. But everyone knows Briana hates her and would do anything to get rid of her."

"Kayla," Luke began hesitantly, his gaze shifting between Maddie and Kayla. "As much as I don't want to admit it, I don't think Briana could have planted them. She arrived after Maddie did."

"Luke's right," Briana chimed in. "I wasn't even here when Maddie could have taken those rings. How could I have possibly set her up?"

The room was silent, everyone absorbing the weight of Briana's words. It was true. Briana had come in after Maddie, griping about Drake needing her to do something for him. And although it pained her to realize, Maddie had no way to prove her innocence.

"Luke?" Maddie whispered, still unable to believe he hadn't defended her. She searched his eyes, desperately seeking understanding or reassurance, but found only uncertainty.

"You know I would never do something like this."

Luke hesitated, his own confusion plain on

his face. "I… I want to believe you, Maddie," he said softly, his gaze flicking toward Briana for a moment. "But the evidence…"

Maddie felt as if an icy hand had closed around her heart, squeezing tightly. The betrayal stung like nothing she had ever experienced before. Of all the people in the room, she thought Luke would be the one to stand by her.

"Fine," she choked out, tears streaming down her cheeks as she turned away from him. "If you don't believe me, then there's nothing more I can say."

"Enough of this," Briana snapped, her voice dripping with disdain. "Claire, I demand that this thief be escorted off the premises immediately."

"Very well," Claire conceded, her expression grave as she motioned for security to approach. "Maddie, I'm sorry, but you'll have to leave."

"Wait," Kayla cried, rushing forward as the guards escorted Maddie toward the door. "Mom, I believe you! I know you didn't steal those things!"

"Thank you," Maddie whispered, her voice cracking with emotion. "I love you."

"I love you too, Mom," Kayla replied, her own eyes shining with tears. "I'm sorry about the other day. I've been a real brat."

"It's okay," Maddie said, putting her arm

around her daughter as they continued toward the door. "We'll figure it out."

But as the door closed behind her with a resounding click, Maddie had no idea how any of this was going to work out. She'd lost Luke, her job, and any hope of being able to hold her head up high in town.

At least things were looking better with Kayla. While Maddie could consider it a victory, it was bittersweet, considering everything else she'd lost.

Luke's boots crunched against the gravel as he walked up to the family ranch house, his heart heavy with guilt and frustration. He couldn't get the image out of his mind of how Maddie had looked at him, begging for his help, and he hadn't been able to come up with anything.

Did he think Maddie capable of stealing? No.

But he also had no reasonable explanation for how the rings could have gotten in Maddie's bag. He'd seen Granny take them off the night before, which was after Briana had left for the night. Briana hadn't returned until after Maddie arrived that morning, so there was no way she could have planted the rings.

"Lord, help me through this," he whispered.

When Luke pushed open the door, a sound coming from upstairs drew his attention.

The house had been locked, and no one should have been in there. Using his military training, he did a quick sweep of the downstairs, making sure no one was there. A few more noises came from above, so he made his way up the stairs, grateful he'd fixed the broken steps so he could move silently.

At the top of the stairs, Granny's bedroom door was ajar. From his vantage point, Luke could see that Granny's jewelry box lay open on her vanity, empty and abandoned, surrounded by a sea of trinkets and keepsakes. And there, kneeling on the floor amidst the chaos, was Drake, Briana's son.

"Drake," Luke called out softly, not wanting to startle the young man. "What are you doing here?"

The boy looked up with wide eyes, a mixture of guilt and fear playing across his features. He tried to hide whatever he was holding behind his back, but it was too late—Luke had seen enough.

"Nothing," Drake stammered, attempting to sound casual. "I was just…looking for something."

"Looking for something?" Luke repeated gently but firmly. "In Granny's things?"

"Yeah," Drake mumbled, avoiding eye contact. "I thought maybe she would want some of her stuff to go with her to the new place."

Given that they'd all been talking to Granny about reducing her belongings to go with her to the nursing home, Luke knew it was a lie.

"Drake," Luke said, taking a step closer to the boy, his tone steady and firm. "Whatever you're hiding, I need you to show it to me. It's important."

"Really, it's nothing," Drake insisted, his face turning a deep shade of crimson. "Just an old ring. I thought… Granny…would like it."

Another lie, because everyone knew that Granny hated all rings, except her wedding rings.

"Please, Drake," Luke implored, his eyes searching the young man's face for any sign of honesty. "I need to know why you're going through Granny's things. It's not like you."

"Fine," Drake conceded, finally revealing the ring he'd been clutching. "But it doesn't matter. It's just a stupid ring. I was just trying to be nice."

"Drake," Luke began, his voice quiet but firm. "I can tell just by looking at it that this ring is too small for Granny. But it looks pretty valuable. Tell me what's really going on. Are you in some kind of trouble?"

Drake's expression shifted to one of panic, his eyes darting between Luke and the door.

"Please," he said. "My mom is already mad at me."

Putting two and two together, Luke asked, "Did you take Granny's wedding rings?"

Tears filled the boy's eyes. "I already gave them back to my mom."

"Why?" Luke asked, trying to keep his own emotions in check as he sought to understand the boy's actions. He'd been right in thinking that Briana hadn't taken the rings, but was it possible that instead of returning them to Granny, she'd slipped them in Maddie's bag to blame her?

"Because..." Drake hesitated, swallowing hard. "Please don't tell my mom and dad. I know you did bad things at my age, so maybe you won't be mad at me the way they will."

Luke felt a rush of sympathy for the young man before him. Whatever trouble the boy was in, he had to be terrified.

"Drake," he said, placing a hand on the boy's shoulder. "I know things have been difficult for all of us lately. But stealing from Granny isn't going to fix anything. How can I help?"

Drake nodded slowly, his eyes filling with tears. "I'm sorry, Luke," he whispered. "Hannah, my girlfriend, is pregnant. I just want to do the right thing, you know? I gotta give her a ring."

The air rushed out of Luke's lungs as he understood what this boy was saying. He'd met Hannah on a number of occasions, and she was a sweet girl. All the things Luke had done wrong, and Drake had the chance to do them right.

"I get it," Luke said. "I know you know about me and Maddie, and…"

Drake nodded. "My mom always says nasty things about her. I don't know what she's going to do when she finds out about Hannah."

Luke held his arms out to the boy. "She's going to love Hannah, and the baby. And we're going to figure this out as a family, okay?"

Even though Drake had never seemed like an affectionate kid, he hugged Luke tight, like he was hanging on for dear life.

From what he'd heard about Brady and his family, they'd accepted Maddie with open arms and given her the support she'd needed for Kayla. Here was Drake, trying to do the same thing.

When they pulled apart, Drake held up the ring. "You think Granny would mind if I gave this to Hannah? Mom used to always say that Granny's rings were for my future wife, but then I heard her yelling about how she overheard Granny telling Maddie that she wanted Maddie to have them when you two got married."

Luke blew out a breath. Maddie. His stomach clenched at the knowledge that he'd been so wrong in not standing up for her. Isn't that what had been their problem to begin with?

He had so much to make up for, but right now, he had to help his cousin's son.

"How about we ask Granny? It's a nice enough

ring, but maybe she'll have something else in mind."

Drake's face fell. "She's gonna be mad at me, too. And here I've been trying to butter her up so she'll give us money for the baby by bringing her treats and things she likes."

One more mystery explained. "You know those treats are making her sick, right?"

Drake looked away, his face flushed with shame. "I… I didn't think it would hurt her," he stammered.

"Granny's health is delicate, and by giving her those things, you're putting her at risk," Luke said. "If you had just talked to her, she'd have understood."

"I just wanted her to love me," Drake whispered, tears welling up in his eyes. "I didn't want her to take away my inheritance and give it to Kayla instead. I'm trying to find a job, but babies are expensive."

Luke sighed, feeling a wave of sympathy for the young man standing before him. How would he have handled it, had he known Maddie was pregnant?

"Listen, Drake," he began softly, placing a hand on the boy's shoulder. "I get it. I'm probably the best person you could have confided in. I promise, no matter what, I'm here for you."

Drake nodded. "Thank you. I'm sorry for trying to steal from Granny. I guess I'm not that good at it. I just hope she can forgive me."

Laughing, Luke said, "Oh, she will. Trust me. Did you ever hear the story about the time I tried to steal from her?"

"No." Drake's eyes widened. "Mom always said you were the black sheep, so I'm surprised she didn't."

"I'll tell you in the car on the way to talk to Granny. Maddie was fired because she was accused of stealing Granny's rings, and you need to make things right. That, and it sounds like we've got a baby to plan for."

Luke put his arm around Drake and began telling him the tale of his own mixed-up youth. Though Luke may have made a mess of his own life, he had hope that he could help someone avoid making the same mistakes. Fixing Drake's damage would be easy enough, but he wasn't so sure he could fix the damage to his relationship with Maddie and Kayla.

Chapter Twelve

Maddie took a deep breath as she stood outside the senior center, her heart pounding in her chest. Claire had texted her, asking her to come in for an urgent meeting, and she couldn't help but assume it was to sign the final papers for her dismissal. A knot settled in her stomach at the thought.

Upon reaching the meeting room, she hesitated for a moment before entering, her heart racing. Maddie's gaze swept over the room, taking in the familiar faces of Luke, Briana, Drake, Kayla, Claire, Eva, and Granny. Her heart ached at the sight of Granny, who looked so small and fragile sitting in her chair.

Even though Maddie had been feeling sorry for herself, she'd been worried about how all of this stress was affecting Granny.

"I'm glad you could join us," Claire said, nodding toward an empty chair beside Granny. "Please have a seat."

Maddie nodded, trying to keep her composure

as she sat down. The air in the room was thick with tension, and she couldn't help but wonder what had brought them all together like this.

"Thank you for joining us, everyone," Luke began, his voice steady but firm. "There's something important we need to discuss."

He paused, then looked at Drake. "I caught Drake stealing from Granny's house, and in our discussion, he admitted to taking the rings Maddie was accused of stealing."

Maddie's eyes widened, and she looked at Drake, who shifted uncomfortably in his seat.

"Drake, what happened to the rings after you took them?" Luke asked, his tone gentle despite the gravity of the situation.

Drake hesitated, his eyes filled with shame. "I… I gave them to my mom," he admitted quietly, his voice cracking.

Maddie felt a mixture of relief and sympathy wash over her, realizing that she'd been called to this meeting because Luke had found a way to exonerate her. And that it had been as she and Kayla had suspected all along.

Briana had set her up.

Briana's face paled at Drake's admission, her eyes darting around the room as if searching for an escape. "That's not true," she stammered, her voice trembling. "I don't know what he's talking about."

"Mom, don't lie!" Drake cried out, his eyes filling with tears. "We all make mistakes, and we have to own them and try to do better. I also was the one who sneaked Granny all those unhealthy things. I was afraid she was going to replace me with Kayla."

Maddie glanced at Granny, who looked genuinely upset at Drake's words. She'd had a lot of harsh things to say about Drake in the past, but hopefully this was making her realize that Drake was simply a boy who needed his Granny's love.

"No one could ever replace you," Granny said. "I keep telling everyone there's enough of me—and my money—to go around."

Maddie reached for Granny's hand, took it and squeezed. Hopefully, this would finally get through to everyone that they didn't need to go to such extreme measures.

"Now it's your turn, Briana," Luke said, giving his cousin a firm look. "Can you please tell everyone what happened?"

Briana stiffened in the chair. "Fine. Drake did take the rings. I was going to return them to Granny, but then I saw Maddie's bag sitting on top of the nurses' station. I was tired of people not listening to me about Maddie's ineptitude, so I...helped things along."

Maddie closed her eyes and said a quick prayer

for patience. Even after all this, Briana was still going on about Maddie.

But that'll serve her right for not taking it directly to her locker. She hadn't intended to leave it unattended, but there was a crisis when she'd arrived, and then she'd gotten distracted, so she had left her bag out for too long.

Luke shook his head. "We need to have this out, once and for all. Maddie has had the patience of a saint dealing with you. Other than not giving you your way, has Maddie ever acted negligently?"

Briana stared at him, openmouthed.

Without letting her answer, he turned his attention to Eva and Claire. "Have any of Briana's complaints against Maddie had any credibility?"

Eva and Claire looked at each other, then shook their heads.

"Until the theft accusation, Maddie's record has been impeccable. Unfortunately, theft is grounds for immediate dismissal," Claire admitted.

The expression on Luke's face could have made him a lawyer. "So since it's been proven that she didn't steal the rings, I'm assuming she has her job back."

Claire nodded. "If she wants it. I feel awful about what happened. I should have done a better investigation."

She turned to Maddie. "I am so sorry. I was a terrible boss, and an even worse friend. Can you forgive me?"

Tears filled Maddie's eyes at the way Claire's voice caught. She didn't know what she'd have done in Claire's position, but she was grateful the truth was out.

"Of course," Maddie said. "And yes, I do want my job back. And the chance to interview for the promotion, if that hasn't already been spoiled."

Luke made a sound. "For what you've been through the past couple of months, you deserve the promotion and more."

Laughing, Claire said, "Agreed. But it's out of my hands, and I will be sure the hiring committee understands that not only were you set up, but you handled the situation with the kind of grace and aplomb that a director should have."

Relief filled Maddie at the idea that her dream might not be out of reach after all.

As Maddie watched the scene unfold before her, a wave of relief washed over her. The truth had finally come to light, exonerating her from any wrongdoing. At the same time, her heart ached for Drake, who had been so desperate for love and attention that he had resorted to such drastic measures.

"Drake," she began, her voice full of compassion. "I'm so sorry we didn't see how much you were hurting. We were all so focused on Kayla and her well-being that we didn't think about how this might be affecting you, too."

Shrugging, Drake said, "I guess I didn't make it easy, either. The truth is, I'm going through some of my own stuff, and I guess I was a little desperate."

Kayla straightened. Then her gaze met Drake's, and she said gently, "Drake, we've never really talked much at school or been friends, but I'd like to change that. We're family now, and it'll be nice to have a cousin my age."

The compassion in Kayla's voice reminded Maddie of how great her daughter could be. They'd talked briefly after Maddie was fired, and though Kayla had apologized, they'd also agreed there was still some work to be done to heal the relationship.

"Maybe," Drake said. "But maybe you'll be embarrassed about me when you find out what I'm going through."

"What could you possibly going through?" Briana scoffed. "You have the perfect life."

Drake shook his head. "No, Mom, I don't. Hannah is pregnant, and I already told her that I'm marrying her and stepping up to be a good father to our baby."

He looked over at Granny. "I'm sorry, Granny. That's why I stole your rings. I was trying to give

Hannah something nice. Luke caught me going through your things to find her a different one, and he said I should just talk to you."

Maddie glanced at Briana, who wore an expression of shock. This probably wasn't what she'd imagined as her son having the perfect life.

"I'm not embarrassed to be friends with you," Kayla said. "It sounds like you're trying to do the right thing and be a father to your baby, like Brady Dad did for me, and like I know Luke Dad would have if he'd known."

Maddie felt a swell of pride as she watched her daughter, sensing the bravery it took for Kayla to reach out to Drake in this difficult moment. Especially because she saw how her daughter's eyes searched for Luke's, like she knew that she had some amends to make there.

"I don't know what to say," Briana finally said.

"I do." Granny stood and went to Drake. "I'm sorry you felt you had to sneak around to do something nice for your future wife. You wouldn't have found anything good at the house, though. I keep all the good stuff in the safety deposit box. We'll make plans to meet there, and you can pick something nice."

She reached forward and hugged her great-grandson. "A baby! We're going to love that baby, and it's going to grow up with family. I hope you know we're here for you."

Maddie teared up at Granny's words. She'd longed to hear those words from her mother, who'd scoffed at her and told her it was her funeral. Having Kayla was the best thing to ever happen to Maddie, even if it had been hard.

Then Granny said, "I only agreed to go to Denver because I wanted to stop all the fighting. But now I want to stay here at the senior center until I'm released to go home. Drake and Hannah need family around them more than ever, so I'm staying."

Eva, who had been silently observing the confrontation, finally cleared her throat. "I must say that I'm disappointed in both of you," she said, looking at Briana and Drake with a stern expression. "But I support Granny's decision to stay at the senior center. It's important for her health and well-being, as well as for the healing of this family."

As the tension in the room seemed to lessen, Briana's posture slumped. "Granny, Maddie, Luke… I'm so sorry," Briana choked out, tears streaming down her cheeks. "I let my jealousy and resentment cloud my judgment, and I acted maliciously. I never meant for any of this to happen."

Then she turned to her son. "I'll admit that being a grandmother so young was never in my plans. But neither was a lot of things, and here we are. Of course we'll be here for you, Hannah, and the baby. I'm sorry I made it so hard for you to tell me."

Maddie reached out and placed a gentle hand on Briana's arm, hoping the warmth of her touch conveyed empathy. "Briana," she began softly, "I understand better than most what it's like to do things you're not proud of."

She hesitated for a moment, feeling the weight of her past actions bearing down on her as she continued, "I lied about who Kayla's father was, and I hurt so many people along the way, but I've come to learn that acting out of fear only brings more trouble into our lives."

As Maddie spoke, Briana's tear-filled eyes met hers, revealing a shared pain. It reminded her a lot of how she and Josie had to work to overcome their painful past, but in the end, they'd figured it out.

Maybe now, Maddie and Briana could move forward in their relationship.

Luke's heart hammered in his chest as he watched Maddie and Briana make peace. He was no stranger to fear—after all, he'd faced it countless times during his military career. But this time, the stakes felt higher, more personal. This wasn't about risking his own life; it was about his relationship with Maddie.

"Since we're all doing the apology thing here," he said, "Maddie, I'm sorry I didn't do more to defend you against Briana's allegations. I knew in my heart that you couldn't have done it, but with the evidence staring us in the face, I didn't know what to say."

He looked over at Kayla. "Even though you still need to learn to do a better job of not blurting out every little thing, I'm glad you stuck up for your mom. I should have done the same."

He gestured at the doorway. "So now that we've gotten all this worked out, let's get Granny to her room so we can unpack and help her settle back in."

As everyone filed out, he stopped Briana. "All that forgiveness stuff, I want to work on that between us, too. We didn't use to hate each other, so let's see if we can find that again."

Briana gave a jerky nod. "I guess maybe I've taken my grudge-holding a little too far. For what it's worth, Corey keeps telling me that, and I suppose I should start listening to him."

The last person out was Maddie, and Luke wanted to believe that perhaps the reason she'd hung back was to talk to him.

"I'm really sorry, Maddie," he said. "I hope someday you can forgive me. I keep using the excuse that I'm new at this, but I feel like it's going to be one of those things I'm constantly trying to get right."

Her smile warmed him all the way to his toes. "I'm pretty sure that's called life. We're all just trying to get it right. I forgive you."

She leaned in and gave him a hug, flooding him with a feeling of safety and comfort.

"I'm so afraid of messing everything up," he admitted. "I've faced death countless times in the army, and I was never so afraid as I am now. I have so much to lose."

Maddie pulled away from their hug and looked up at him. "I'm scared, too. I nearly lost everything, and yet it all worked out. I have to believe that God has had His hand on our lives, guiding us, especially when things look the bleakest."

"So what you're saying is we'll figure it out."

Smiling at him, she said, "It hasn't failed me yet."

Though he'd thought Kayla had left, she came around the corner and said, "If you two are serious about facing your fears, then maybe it's time to work on the fears you have about each other and your relationship."

He recognized the look of irritation on Maddie's face. And this time, he had it covered.

"You trying to tell us what to do didn't end well for the three of us the last time. Just like we have to trust in God and each other to work through things, you have to trust that your mom and I are going to figure that out, too."

Kayla's shoulders slumped slightly. "Is it so wrong to want you two to be happy?"

"That's on us, not you," Maddie said gently. "We both get it. Now you need to stop."

For the first time, Kayla looked contrite. "I'm sorry. Brady Dad also said I was out of line. I'll try to do better."

"Kayla's right," Granny piped up. "You two belong together. I've seen the way you care for each other and how you both light up when you're around one another. There's something special between you, and it would be a shame not to give it a chance."

"Maybe you're both right," Maddie said, her gaze shifting between Luke, Kayla, and Granny. "We've been so focused on our own fears and insecurities that we haven't given our relationship the opportunity it deserves."

For a moment, all was quiet in the hallway as the weight of their daughter's words settled over them. Luke took a deep breath, realizing that as much as he'd thought he had at stake, they did have family members who also wanted to see them happy.

"Yes, but this is our relationship," Luke emphasized. "You two have to let us figure it out ourselves. No more meddling. Got it?"

Even though Kayla and Granny exchanged conspiratorial looks before nodding, Luke would accept that as a yes.

Then he looked up at Maddie, her eyes shining. She'd never looked so beautiful, and even though the nursing home was not the most romantic spot for their first official kiss as a couple, he pulled her back into the now-empty conference room, closing the door so Granny and Kayla couldn't see in.

"What is this about?" Maddie asked.

"Just that I want to seal our newfound relationship with a kiss, and I don't want those two nosy Nellies spying on us."

Maddie nodded, her eyes full of light as she gazed back at him. And somehow, in that moment, all Luke's fears dissipated.

Slowly, Luke leaned down and captured Maddie's lips with his own. The kiss was sweet and tender, speaking to the promise of the future together as a very large and unusual family. But family, nonetheless. And he was so grateful to Maddie for showing him that family truly was what you made it.

Epilogue

Maddie couldn't help but smile as she looked around the table in Granny's newly fixed-up house, her heart swelling with gratitude and love for everyone gathered there.

"Thank you all so much," Granny began, her voice thick with emotion. "I can't tell you how wonderful it is to be back in my own home, surrounded by my family. Your support during my recovery has meant the world to me."

Maddie felt tears prick at the corners of her eyes as she listened to Granny's heartfelt words. She knew just how important this moment was—not only for Granny but for every person sitting around that table. They'd all worked so hard to get her home.

As the meal came to an end, laughter and lighthearted chatter filled the air while they all helped clear the table, everyone rushing a little more than usual. Granny had finally been cleared by her doctor to ride again, and they were all looking forward to going to the stables so they could have a family horseback ride.

Ordinarily, they'd have had the family meal at Shepherd's Creek, but given that this was their first meal with Granny being released, they wanted to do it at her house.

"Granny, I can't wait to see you back in the saddle," Maddie said, glad she could finally encourage Granny in her passion.

Luke's eyes met Maddie's from across the room, a warm smile playing on his lips. Their gazes held for a moment longer than necessary, hinting at the connection between them.

The best part about waiting so long to have a romance was that she felt they both were committed to doing things right, which strengthened their bond.

"Are you all ready to head out?" Brady asked, addressing the group. The excitement in his voice was contagious as he glanced back at Maddie, who couldn't help but grin back at him.

Once more, she was so grateful that they'd been able to have such a deep friendship in spite of their past.

"Yes!" Kayla chimed in, her eyes sparkling with anticipation. "I've been waiting for this day forever!"

They all loaded into their respective vehicles for the short drive to the stables. It was a little inconvenient, but it was well worth it to give Granny the chance to have her first family meal in her own home.

Once they arrived at the stables, Maddie noticed Briana and her husband, Corey, along with Drake and Hannah, lingering behind. They appeared hesitant, their eyes darting back and forth between the group and the horses. Maddie knew they weren't as familiar or comfortable with the animals as the rest of them were.

"Hey, guys," Kayla called out, a friendly smile on her face. "You should join us. It's going to be so much fun!"

Hannah patted her growing belly. "I'm going to sit this one out. Josie and I are due around the same time, and she was going to give me some tips on what else I need for the baby."

It warmed Maddie's heart that the young girl had someone who could be a mentor to her as she navigated these changes in her life. Maddie hadn't had that, and in a way, having the family be there to support Drake and Hannah felt like a redemption of her own story.

"What about you? Come on, Briana! Drake! Corey!" Kayla's encouragement made Maddie smile.

"Thanks, Kayla," Briana responded hesitantly, glancing at her husband and son. "But we're not really…horse people."

"Aw, don't worry about it," Kayla reassured them, her voice sweet and encouraging. "We can all help you. I promise, it's not as scary as it seems."

Drake's face lit up as he walked over to Kayla. "Honestly, I've always wanted to learn more about horses."

"Me, too," Corey said, joining them. "Funny how you live in the country, and you're surrounded by animals you don't know much about."

Having Briana and her family join theirs seemed like a natural progression of the Shepherd's Creek group. Somehow, they'd all managed to make everything fit together, and it was working better than Maddie could have imagined.

"What about you, Briana?" Kayla asked.

"Thank you," Briana said, her voice softening. "But I think I'll just stick to taking pictures for now. I want to capture all these beautiful memories for Granny."

As the laughter and chatter continued around them, Maddie caught Luke's gaze from across the yard. The warmth emanating from his eyes sent shivers down her spine, and she couldn't possibly imagine herself loving anyone more.

Loving Luke had been worth the wait.

"Hey, Maddie," Luke called out to her, walking closer with a soft smile playing on his lips.

He looked around at their gathered family, then back at her.

"You act like you're up to something," she said. "If this is another one of Wyatt's water balloon fights, I will get you all. Kayla did my hair so nice for today."

Now that Kayla had agreed to let Maddie and Luke's relationship be what it needed to be, mother and daughter had found a new closeness. Today, Kayla had even offered to do Maddie's hair, saying it would be fun to dress up for Granny's special dinner.

Of course, they'd all soon be covered in dust, but Maddie wasn't going to have it ruined by the guys and one of their silly pranks.

"And it does look beautiful," Luke said. "But you know I think you're beautiful no matter how your hair looks."

She smiled at him, feeling so loved by this man. Now that everyone had given them a little space to explore their relationship, she was learning to feel secure in his love.

"So you might notice that everyone is here for Granny, but they're also here for another occasion."

Maddie looked around, noticing that everyone had gathered in a sort of semicircle.

"Oh? What's the occasion?"

Luke grinned and bent on one knee, holding

out an engagement ring. "Will you marry me, Maddie?"

Tears welled up in Maddie's eyes as she processed the enormity of his question. Sure, she'd known they were eventually going to get to this place, but having him ask her, here, in front of everyone they'd loved, it seemed almost too much to process.

The people gathered represented so much of their lives, the past they regretted, the things they'd done wrong and made right, but also a present, where they'd learned to support each other. More importantly, as she felt the love from everyone gathered, she saw the hope of the future, and was secure in the knowledge that together, with God's help, they could get through anything.

"Yes," Maddie said.

As Luke rose and kissed her, she could hear Kayla in the background.

"Finally!" she exclaimed. "I knew you two were meant for each other. We're going to be a real family now!"

Maddie and Luke exchanged a tender smile as laughter bubbled up from everyone around them.

"It's about time," Granny said as they pulled apart. "We've got a wedding to plan!"

"Wait, wait!" Briana called out, holding up her phone. "I got it all on video! I can't wait to share our family's happy news with everyone."

"Thank you, Briana," Maddie said, touched by the sincerity of her words. She wouldn't call Briana her best friend, but at least they'd finally become friends.

"Let's come together," Luke encouraged them, spreading his arms wide to invite everyone into a group hug. They all stepped closer, wrapping their arms around one another, symbolizing the bond they now shared despite their past mistakes and misunderstandings.

Maddie would have never imagined, as the little girl who loved being here at the stables, but always felt like she didn't belong, that this was now her home, and this was now her family.

And she'd found a love in Luke that she'd never dreamed possible, but with God's hand on them all, was hers to cherish.

* * * * *

Dear Reader,

Believe it or not, this letter has been the hardest part of writing this book. Do I tell you how we lost a good friend, Luke, and one of our horses, Stolley Bear, shortly before I started writing this book, and how every scene with Stolley Bear was a real scene that happened with our horse? Or do I tell you that Maddie's story has been with me from day one, because even the town bad girl deserves a chance at redemption? Well, I guess I just told you both.

So many of my stories are about the power of redemption and God's love. This one was no different. Maddie's story is important because I think in some ways, many of us have that story. We've done something wrong in our past that keeps haunting us, even though God forgave us a long time ago. Like Maddie, I hope you learn to give yourself the same forgiveness that God gives you.

God's blessings to you and yours,
Danica Favorite